LOST CHILDREN OF THE FAR ISLANDS

CHILDREN

OF THE

FAR ISLANDS

EMILY RAABE

ALFRED A. KNOPF
NEW YORK

For my family, who always believed.

THIS IS A BORZOI BOOK PUBLISHED BY ALFRED A. KNOPF

Text copyright © 2014 by Emily Raabe
Jacket art copyright © 2014 by Manuel Šumberac

All rights reserved. Published in the United States by Alfred A. Knopf, an imprint of Random House Children's Books, a division of Random House LLC, a Penguin Random House Company, New York.

Knopf, Borzoi Books, and the colophon are registered trademarks of Random House LLC.

Visit us on the Web! randomhouse.com/kids

Educators and librarians, for a variety of teaching tools, visit us at RHTeachersLibrarians.com

Library of Congress Cataloging-in-Publication Data
Raabe, Emily.
Lost children of the far islands / Emily Raabe. — First edition.
p. cm.
Summary: After their mother falls mysteriously ill, eleven-year-old twins Gus and Leo and their mute younger sister, Ila, learn that they share their mother's ability to transform into animals, and to defeat the evil King of the Black Lakes, they must harness this newfound power.
ISBN 978-0-375-87091-0 (trade) — ISBN 978-0-375-97091-7 (lib. bdg.) —
ISBN 978-0-307-97497-6 (ebook)
[1. Supernatural—Fiction. 2. Shapeshifting—Fiction. 3. Brothers and sisters—Fiction. 4. Family life—Maine—Fiction. 5. Selective mutism—Fiction. 6. Adventure and adventurers—Fiction. 7. Maine—Fiction.] I. Title.
PZ7.R10033Los 2014
[Fic]—dc23
2013014768

The text of this book is set in 13-point Goudy Old Style.

Printed in the United States of America

April 2014

10 9 8 7 6 5 4 3 2 1

First Edition

CONTENTS

Out of the cradle of solitude
the rocking vessel carries you
out of the cold rain and stone jetties
the steepled firs lost in fog
out of the meadows of vetch and rue
the wilting buttercups—
it is never easy leaving the island

From "Leaving the Island,"
Alison Hawthorne Deming

CHAPTER 1

Illness in the House

• MAINE •

On May 23, exactly one month before Gustavia and Leomaris Brennan's eleventh birthday, their mother became terribly, mysteriously ill.

At first, it was quite a wonderful day. For one thing, it was a Saturday, which meant sleeping in, at least for Leo. Gus could never sleep in, so she hopped out of bed at her usual time and ran down to the kitchen, where she found her father mixing batter for pancakes.

"Morning," Gus said. Her dad murmured back as he peered into his mixing bowl. Ila said nothing, but she smiled up at Gus from her bowl of oatmeal, the only breakfast she would eat.

"Where's Mom?" Gus asked.

"Not feeling well," her father said lightly. "I figured I'd let her sleep. I don't have to go into the lab today anyway. Let's go wake up that brother of yours."

Ila jumped up and grabbed her bowl of oatmeal off the table to follow them.

"Food at the table, Ila," their father said. Ila gave him her *Please?* smile, and he shook his head in defeat. "OK, but two hands and no juice."

Ila gave a happy little hop, which made Gus and her father laugh, and they progressed as a group to Leo's room.

Gus shoved the door open. Leo was asleep. Leo loved to sleep almost as much as he loved to read books.

Except for their looks, Gus and Leo were as different as twins could be. Gus didn't hate reading; she just didn't have time for it. She was happiest when she was moving. She liked to run, and was the only fifth grader on the Girls A soccer team. But what she really loved was swimming. Gus swam on the school's club team in the winter, and on the town team in the summer. She loved the smell of the water, the salt of the ocean, even the chlorine smell of the school pool. As soon as she got in the water, everything else faded. In the pool she was not the smart Brennan's sister, or the sister of the Brennan who never spoke. She was simply the fastest swimmer.

Leo swam too, but while Gus was winning her races, he was usually ruining a library book by the edge of the pool. Their mother always said that if he could only figure out how to read in his sleep, Leo would be perfectly happy for the rest of his life. As it was, he usually settled for reading himself to sleep, which he had clearly done the night before. He was lying on his side with his face mashed into the book that lay open on his pillow. His glasses were half on and half off, tilted at the crazy angle they had slipped to in the night.

"Leo!" Gus said.

"Humph." Leo did not move.

"Dad's making pancakes, Leo!"

At this, Leo opened one eye, dark brown, almost black, like Gus's. Leo and Gus took after their mother, who was small and slender with glossy dark hair and coffee-colored eyes. Ila's curly red hair and oddly colored eyes were her own. They appeared to be brown, the same dark shade as Leo's and Gus's, but a closer look revealed a starburst of incandescent green at the center of each one. Looking into Ila's eyes was dizzying.

"Where's Mom?" Leo asked, sitting up and sliding his glasses back onto his nose. His hair stood up so that he looked like a hedgehog in danger. His book thumped to the floor.

"Under the weather," their father said. "You're stuck with me."

Leo grinned and pushed his hair away from his face, which resulted in it sticking even farther up in the air.

"Pancakes," he said approvingly.

Their mother stayed in bed all day.

"She must be really sick," Gus said to Leo. They were playing chess on an old wooden board on the living room floor. Ila was alternating between looking at her favorite book, one about a frog and a toad that were best friends, and playing with her stuffed bear, dressing and undressing it and leading it on soundless adventures across the rug.

Gus and Leo's sister was a little bit weird. Well, really, a lot weird. For one thing, she didn't talk. It wasn't that she was quiet or slow to respond, but that she didn't talk at all. Ila was five years old, but she had never spoken a word. She was also what their mother called *sensitive*. Although Ila couldn't—or wouldn't—speak, she definitely could scream. When she was a baby, it seemed like anything would make her scream: being wrapped too tightly in her blankets, or being woken suddenly, or the one—and only—time Gus had been allowed to feed her from her bottle.

"It's not you," her mother had said as she plucked the writhing, shrieking baby from Gus's arms. "The milk was too cold—that's all, Gussy. Not you."

Gus was hurt anyway. She had been waiting with huge excitement for the new baby. She and Leo were five when Ila arrived. Leo had taken a good look at her and wandered away, but Gus loved her from the start. When Ila had first peered up at her with her strange, beautiful eyes, Gus could barely breathe. Her own sister.

But the baby, it turned out, was not really that much fun. For one thing, she cried all the time. Anything abrupt—a light flicked on in a dark room, a siren going by, even the bang of a door closing—would make

Ila panic. Her small face would turn bright red, her eyes would squinch shut, and then she would start screaming.

"She's just a little overwhelmed," their father had said. But it was more than that. It was as if Ila had keener senses than the rest of them and was being bombarded by the world at its regular, human-made level. For instance, Gus was pretty sure Ila could see in the dark. She never bothered to turn the lights on in their room, not even at night. Gus liked to believe that her little sister, having lost so much by not speaking, had gained in other areas.

"She also has better hearing than any of us," she pointed out to her father. "Remember when the Browns' cat went missing and Ila was the one who found him in the closet in the spare room? Nobody else could hear him meowing."

"That's just because she's so quiet herself," her father said, but Gus thought he looked pleased at the thought of his youngest having gifts instead of merely the deficit of silence. .

As Ila got older, her tantrums lessened. But Mrs. Destito, the nurse practitioner at the clinic, was concerned about the Brennans' youngest child. Since it was difficult to bring Ila to her office, where the strange noises and bright lights could set her off, she had sent a young woman to their house to examine her. A behavior specialist, she called herself. She had a high-pitched voice that went up even higher when she spoke to Ila. It sounded like she was talking to a puppy.

"Such an interesting name," the woman said in her puppy voice. "What in the world does it mean, I wonder?"

"It means *island*," their mother said shortly.

" 'Island,' " the woman said. "How very, mmm, odd."

No one said anything. What was there to say to such a rude comment?

"Now, *Ila*," the woman had crooned, "show me your nice bear?" When she said *bear*, she stretched the word out so that it sounded like two long words, the second one a question.

They were in the living room, having tea and cookies. Ila, who was three at the time, was playing on the rug with the first of her many bears. She ignored the woman.

"Ila," their father said, "say hello to the nice lady." His voice gave away what he really thought of the nice lady. Ila ignored him as well.

"Hmmm," the woman said, making a note in the spiral notebook that she pulled out of a large canvas bag. The bag also held toys, which she offered, one by one, to Ila. Ila ignored them all in favor of her bear, who was now practicing headstands on the living room rug.

After a while, Leo drifted out, no doubt to go to his room to read or to continue training his turtles, one of whom he claimed could pick between a blue string and a red string almost 100 percent of the time. Gus had stayed, sitting quietly on one end of the couch, hoping not to be asked to leave. Gus loved listening in on adults' conversations, even when they were boring. And she sensed that this conversation, while slightly boring at the moment, was very important.

The behavior specialist had been talking at great length about something called early intervention.

"With the right training," she said, leaning forward as she spoke, "Ila can even learn to interact with regularly-abled children!" She sounded delighted at her own prediction. "We will need to do more testing, of course, to see where Ila falls—"

"No," their mother interrupted.

The woman looked startled.

"I'm sorry," their mother said, "but I've been doing a fair amount of research, and Ila just doesn't fit the profile. She makes perfect eye contact, for example. And she plays with Gus and Leo, doesn't she, Peter?"

Her voice rose just a bit as she said his name. Their father put an arm around her shoulders. Ila played quietly at their feet. Gus sat as still as possible.

"She makes eye contact!" their mother said again. She sounded like she might cry. "She's just—quiet. Quiet and a bit sensitive. We don't want her subjected to any more testing. We—"

The woman leaned forward again, and Gus's mother stopped speaking. "Ila," the woman said, and her voice was suddenly quite normal. "Can you come over here, Ila?"

The room went very still. Gus found herself holding her breath as she waited for her little sister to respond.

Go on, Ila! she wanted to say, but she forced herself to keep quiet.

Ila looked up at the behavior specialist, her eyes shining in the light from the lamp behind the couch. She smiled and waved one chubby hand.

Their mother said—and now she really was crying—"You see! Well done, Ila! Go on over, honey."

Ila obediently toddled over to the woman, who scooped her up. Gus braced herself, but Ila seemed content to sit on the woman's lap. She examined the string of pearls that the woman wore around her neck. Everyone in the room relaxed. Gus's mother wiped her eyes. But then the woman made the mistake of pulling a tiny penlight from her shirt pocket and shining it in Ila's eyes, making the starbursts at the center of them glow a dangerous, vivid green.

"What unusual eyes! I'm just going to track her pupils," the woman said brightly, shining the light back and forth. Ila's face grew pink, and then red.

"Oh dear," their father said. The corners of his mouth twitched.

Gus clamped her hands over her ears just as Ila shrieked and pulled away from the woman, who made the second mistake of taking hold of her wrists.

When it was all over—the spilled tea mopped up, the crushed cookies swept, the lamp put right, and the behavior specialist shown politely but firmly to her car—their father had called a family meeting.

"Your sister is just fine," he'd said sternly, looking from Gus to Leo and back to Gus. Ila was in bed, having exhausted herself with screaming. "There will be no more talk of this ism or that ism," their father continued.

"Ila is who she is," their mother added, "and that's final."

Gus and Leo looked at one another, bewildered. They had decided a long time ago that their weird little sister was just that—their weird little sister. Why talk about it more?

"Duh, Dad," Leo said finally.

"Personally," Gus said, "I think Leo's weirder than Ila. I mean, he trains turtles."

"They're very underrated," Leo said complacently. "It's clear from Ditmars's *Reptiles of the World* that they have much more complicated family structures than most people think."

Gus looked pointedly at their father.

"Well, OK, then," he said, throwing up his hands. "Let's have some lunch."

As it turned out, Ila did have to have more testing, but none of the tests ever turned up anything actually wrong with her, other than her silence. In the end it was decided that she had something called selective mutism, which meant that she could understand language perfectly well and could, and probably would, speak someday. Her sensitivity to lights and noise decreased as she got older. She went to kindergarten, and her teacher admitted that she seemed to be learning everything along with the other children. She'll talk when she is ready, their parents said, and so, for the time being anyway, that was that.

If they had lived in a bigger town, Ila might have been teased, or worse. But in their tiny town, where everybody knew everyone else, she was simply known as the Brennans' quiet child, in much the same way that Gus was known as the fastest swimmer on the team and Leo as a bookworm.

Leo was also frustratingly good at chess. Luckily, he rarely paid attention long enough to beat Gus.

"Mmm," said Leo now, moving a horse. He was not looking at the board. Behind him, Ila laid her bear on the rug and tucked a blanket around it for bedtime.

"Leo!" Gus scolded him. "That leaves your king open!"

"Sorry," Leo said, moving the horse back. "I was reading this cool book about wolves last night. I was just thinking about pack families. Did you know, Gus—"

"Whatever," Gus said. "Just *go*."

Leo slid a pawn forward, saying, as if Gus had not interrupted him, "So then the alpha female—the mother wolf—*pukes* up her food for the cubs—"

Gus sighed. "Check," she said, and took his queen.

Their mother came down for dinner. Her face was pale and she had dark circles under her eyes, as if she had been sick for weeks rather than just one day.

"Feeling better, Rosie?" their father asked gently, and

she murmured, "Oh yes, thanks, darling," as she took her seat, folding into the chair.

All through dinner she was remote and tense. When the wind banged a shutter at the back of the house, she actually jumped from her chair with a slight scream. Their father was up and at her side immediately.

"Rosemaris," he said, and then when she did not answer him but continued to look wildly about her, as if expecting intruders to burst into the kitchen, he said, "Rosie! It's just the wind. It's fine."

"I'm sorry," their mother said. "I'm just a little tired, I think."

"How're the tides, Dad?" Leo asked, pushing up his glasses on his nose.

Their father was a physical oceanographer. He studied something called Alexandrium cells, which are organisms that cause the algal blooms known as red tides in the Gulf of Maine. Red tides, he had explained, are dangerous because the algae can build up in the tissues of shellfish, poisoning them.

But in the last month, their father had been pulled off the red tide project to study a new problem—the tide markers in the Gulf of Maine were showing unusually high tides. The phenomenon was erratic, happening only every few days or so, but it was troubling.

"Still happening," their father answered Leo. "It's really strange. There doesn't seem to be a pattern to them."

"But it could be underwater earthquakes, right?" Gus asked.

"Well, it could be, but it's not very likely."

"What about a tsunami?" Leo said eagerly. "Starting small, you know, way deep, and just building, building, building." He crept his hand along the table to demonstrate. "Then, *whoosh!*" He reached over to Ila, who was watching his approaching wave hand with fascination, and tickled her, making her giggle.

"It's not funny, Leo," their mother said, her voice unusually sharp.

Their father gave her a look and said in a softer voice, "It's probably related to global warming. We're looking into the melting ice at the polar caps as a possible cause. But even if that is the case, there's only about a one—"

"I know," Leo said gloomily. "A one-in-a-thousand chance of a tsunami ever hitting Maine."

"Cheer up," their father said, grinning at Leo. "Maybe we'll have a bad hurricane season."

"What about those missing fishing boats?" Gus asked.

Their father stopped smiling. Three fishing boats had been lost in the Gulf of Maine since April. All three had gone down during freak storms that had risen out of the sea with no warning and then vanished as quickly as they had come. No traces of the boats, or of the fishermen who had been aboard them, had been found.

"Nothing," he said very quietly.

"But fishing accidents have always happened, right, Dad?" Gus said.

Their father nodded, but his expression was grim.

"Yes, but not like this. Maybe two, three incidents a year, but not three boats in one spring. That's nine men missing now."

Their mother stood up abruptly, her chair squeaking as she shoved it away from the table. "I'm going back to bed," she said. "Peter?"

Their father got up quickly and took her arm, helping her to the stairs as if she were an old woman. As they went upstairs, the children could just hear their mother's voice.

"You'll only frighten them," she was saying.

"I'm not scared," Leo said. "Are you, Ila?"

Ila shook her head firmly, her red curls bouncing against her cheeks.

"But Mom is," Gus said. "It probably reminds her . . ." Her voice trailed off. They all knew the story of their mother's family, although it was never spoken about. Her parents had drowned in a boating accident when she was just seventeen. Rosemaris had been on the boat as well, but was saved when a boy, out fishing early in the morning during his vacation from college, found her clinging to a lobster buoy. She was half dead from hypothermia, but she survived. She had no other family, so the boy's parents took her in. She waited tables at LuLu's Diner until the boy finished college, and then they were married. A year later, they had twin babies. They named the girl Gustavia, after the boat that Peter had been driving when he found the half-drowned girl. Leo's full name was Leomaris, which means *lion of the sea*, something that Leo pretended to be embarrassed by but secretly thought was pretty cool.

"Maybe," Leo said, suddenly thoughtful. "I mean, it is kind of weird, you know, that they haven't found any wreckage or anything, right? It's a little freaky."

"Charlotte says her dad hasn't been taking his lobster boat out," Gus said. "Her mom won't let him. She says they've been fighting like crazy about it, 'cause you know they have to pay for that special school for her little brother, and they're going to run out of money if he doesn't go out."

"Well, freak storms are, by definition, anomalies," Leo said. He reached for the bread plate. Since there were no grown-ups at the table to stop him, he jammed two pieces into his mouth and then followed them with a spoonful of butter. "I'm thure it will all be thine," he said.

"Gross," Gus said. "Gross, gross, gross."

"Yum," Leo said as Ila grinned delightedly.

But it wasn't fine. In fact, it got worse quickly after that.

CHAPTER 2

Swimming Underwater

As the days went by, their mother seemed to withdraw further and further until she was no longer *there*, in some sort of indefinable way. Her face grew thinner, and her gaze more remote. Gus felt like shaking her just to see if she would notice her daughter standing in front of her. At first, Gus was angry with her mother. But by the second week of her illness, she wasn't angry anymore. She was frightened.

When the three children came home after school, their mother was usually in her studio. She was a quite famous painter. Her work sold all over the world. The paintings were always of the same subject, shining flat and green in sunlight, kicking up white splashes in the wind, churning with black waves in a storm. The Brennans' backyard sloped down to rock ledges and then to the sea. Their mother's studio had an uninterrupted view from its long windows, so that she could stand at her easel and paint the changing ocean landscape.

But these days, although she was in her studio, she was not working. Instead, she simply sat in the rocking chair at the window, staring out at the Atlantic Ocean where it curled and broke and sprayed below the yard.

"She's just trying to work out some problem in her head with that new painting," their father explained. "It's a big deal, you know."

"I know," Gus muttered impatiently. "But, Dad, she wouldn't even tell me if I could go to Anna's Friday night. I mean, can't she just snap out of it and let me know if I can have an overnight?"

"I'll call Anna's mom," her dad said. "But, Gus, you have to promise me that you're not going to talk to Anna, or Anna's parents, about Mom being sick."

"I already told her Mom was sick," Gus said irritably. "She's my best friend!"

"Well, please don't tell her any more about it," her dad said. "It's just a family matter, and I don't want you talking about it with anyone outside the family."

"But—" Gus began.

Her father interrupted her. "You need to respect your mom's privacy, Gus. If you can't promise me, then I can't let you go."

Gus wasn't even sure she wanted to go to Anna's house anymore. She and Anna told each other everything. And her dad was making her feel weird, like she shouldn't be having an overnight at all, like her mom was really sick or something.

But all she said was "Fine. I promise," and stomped off to her room.

Then Friday the strangeness at the swim meet happened, and Gus forgot all about her overnight at Anna's. Gus and Leo were both fast in the water, although Gus won more races than Leo. Leo wasn't really interested in winning. He got distracted easily, and was always getting disqualified for diving in before the start.

Gus's last race was the hundred-meter breaststroke, which she won easily. Gus's secret goal was to swim in the Olympics someday. No one knew that, not even her coach. He had told her he thought she could win the individual medley at States the next year if she kept working hard, and she had, but she had bigger things in mind than States.

Gus and Anna wrapped themselves up together in Anna's giant beach towel and stood at the side of the pool to watch the boys' race. They arranged their feet so that underneath their towel it was white foot, brown foot, white foot, brown foot. They always did this, and it always made them giggle.

The race began, and this time Leo dove in at the right time.

"Good start!" Anna shouted, clapping. Gus laughed, but Anna was serious. Anna had a crush on Leo, a fact that Gus did her best to ignore.

Leo was neck and neck underwater with David Lee, who was the fastest swimmer on the boys' team. But when David's head broke the surface, he was alone. Gus thought Leo must have fallen behind, but then she saw the dark blur under the surface, out in front. A few of Leo's friends were screaming his name, but most of the spectators didn't seem to realize that there was a boy under the water, leading the race. They were screaming David Lee's name.

"What in the world is he doing?" Anna said into Gus's ear, but Gus had no answer.

The crowd was now shouting Leo's name as he touched the far wall and turned without coming up for a breath. Anna was screaming too, jumping so vigorously that the towel fell off, leaving the two of them wet and cold in their racing suits. Anna didn't notice because she was too excited. Gus didn't notice either, but it was not out of excitement. She was watching her brother intently. Leo's head finally broke the surface as he touched the wall, breathing hard, his hair sleek and wet.

He won, but of course he was disqualified for not swimming the right stroke. That didn't stop his teammates from swamping him, yelling and cheering and slapping him on the back.

Leo glanced up from the huddle around him and caught Gus's eye. His expression was that of a rabbit surrounded by hounds. So Gus waded in and hauled him away by one arm, past teammates begging to know how he had done it and when he was going to show them how to hold their breath for that long.

"Late for family dinner," Gus said loudly, keeping a firm grip on Leo.

"Thanks," he said as they hustled out to the hallway, dodging other swimmers. Gus saw their coach heading their way. His expression was purposeful and not at all pleased.

"Quick," she told Leo. "Outside." So they ducked out a side door into the parking lot of the school, their bare feet slapping the blacktop. Gus pulled sweatshirts out of the canvas bag that held their clothes. They yanked them on over their wet suits, and then hopped into blue jeans, Leo tugging his awkwardly over his suit. Their feet were too wet for socks, so they just shoved their sneakers on.

They walked the few blocks home without speaking. Gus was waiting for Leo to say something, to explain what had happened back there, but he seemed lost in his own world. This was not unusual for Leo, but it was irritating. Finally, as they reached the driveway, Gus couldn't stand it.

"What were you doing?" she said. She stopped and pulled on Leo's sleeve, so that he had to face her. "How did you do that?"

Leo shrugged. "I dunno." He tugged his arm free and started up the driveway.

"Have you been practicing?" Gus persisted, following Leo. "Have you been, like, holding your breath in the tub or something? Tell me, Leo!"

Leo stopped and spun around. His face was pale and

angry. "I don't know!" he said. "OK? I have no idea what happened. It just did. And to tell you the truth, it freaked me out a little. I wanted to come up, Gus. I started to level out, you know, to come up for air, and I *couldn't*. I just . . . couldn't."

"What do you mean, you couldn't? Leo, what do you mean, you couldn't come up?"

But Leo pulled free, and taking the three steps to the porch in one jump, he yanked open the front door and was gone into the house. The door banged shut behind him.

Gus followed him in. She felt a bit frightened, and a bit annoyed as well. Honestly, wasn't it enough that their mom was acting so weird? Did they really need Leo to be weird as well? She slammed the door behind her.

"Don't slam the door!" her mother called from the kitchen. She sounded so normal that Gus relaxed a little bit.

In the kitchen, Ila and her parents were sitting around the old farmhouse table eating pizza.

"I thought you were going to Anna's," Gus's dad said to her.

"Oh shoot!" Gus had completely forgotten that she was supposed to go to Anna's after the swim meet. "I'll call her right now." She went to the living room to grab the phone, saying over her shoulder, "Save me some plain slices!"

Gus called Anna and apologized. She dodged her

questions about the swim meet by saying simply that Leo had been practicing holding his breath for months, and it was just a prank.

Back in the kitchen, she slid into her chair and grabbed a slice of plain pizza. Across the table, Ila was picking the pineapple off her pizza and giving it to Leo, who was adding it to his slice. Ila never ate the pineapple pieces, but she always chose the pineapple slices of pizza, and would turn up her nose at any other kind. It was a mystery to her family, like so many things about Ila.

"Did you tell them?" Gus asked.

Leo shot her a look.

"Tell us what?" their dad said. "You two won everything and are leaving us to train for the next Olympics?"

"Ha ha," Gus said. "No, about swimming underwater."

"It doesn't matter," Leo said through a mouthful of pizza.

"Don't talk with your mouth full," their mother said automatically.

Leo swallowed noisily. "It was stupid." He stuffed another bite of pizza into his mouth.

"You mean *weird*," Gus said. "Leo swam the entire one hundred underwater," she explained to her parents. "He just went under and stayed under until the end. It was actually kind of amazing," she admitted.

"What do you mean, underwater?" their mother said.

She didn't sound amazed. She sounded upset, almost angry. "Leo, what happened?"

"Mahthong," Leo said, and then chewed and swallowed and started again. "Nothing. I just—I just stayed under, that's all. I didn't even want to, really. I mean, I didn't do it deliberately or anything. It just happened."

"You didn't need to breathe?" Their mother had risen to her feet and was standing with her hands flat on the table, leaning toward Leo. "Not at all? Think carefully, Leo. You never needed to breathe, the whole time?"

"No," Leo said, sounding a little frightened. "What's the big deal?"

Their mother looked at their father, and something unspoken traveled between them.

"Why don't you sit down, Rosemaris," their father said gently. And very slowly, she did.

"Sorry, sweetheart," she said to Leo. "It sounds funny—I'll bet your teammates were surprised!" Her voice was light, but her face looked drawn and strained.

No one said anything for a long moment. Their mom stood up again. "I'm just going upstairs for a bit," she said, and without another word, she left the table.

They ate in silence for a few minutes, and then their dad sighed and stood up also. "Plates in the sink when you're done, kids. I'm going to check on your mom."

They heard his heavy steps on the stairs. Leo said, "Well, I guess we can eat as much as we want," and went back for thirds. "Ila, do you want another piece?"

Ila shook her head.

"Let's do jammies and teeth, Ila," Gus said. She pushed away her uneaten second piece of pizza.

Ila brushing her teeth was a mixture of boring and infuriating. She had to do the toothpaste herself, and it had to be an exact amount that stretched from one end of the bristles to the other. If the squeeze of toothpaste fell short, or if she squeezed out a bit too much, then she started the whole thing over. And she brushed each tooth separately. Gus's mom said that she probably learned it in kindergarten. Gus didn't care where she learned it. It was annoying.

"Please, Ila, not again," she begged as Ila held the toothbrush at eye level and scrutinized the toothpaste, which extended beyond the edge of the brush by just a hair. Ignoring Gus, Ila scraped the offending toothpaste into the sink and began again.

"Argh!" Gus said. "And, Leo, cut it out!" she yelled into the hallway.

Leo was in his bedroom, practicing his trumpet. Leo loved his trumpet and practiced every day, but in spite of that, he was a terrible player. Gus saw their father come out of the master bedroom and walk down the hall toward them. She figured he would ask Leo to torture them all another time, but he walked right past Leo's room and came into the bathroom.

"Gussy, can you get Ila into bed tonight?" he asked. His eyes were red, as if he had been crying.

"Sure," Gus said quickly. "Just make Leo stop the squawking."

"Of course," he said absently. "Of course. Thanks, honey."

He kissed Ila, who was finally finished with the interminable brushing, and then patted Gus on her shoulder and drifted back out of the room.

"OK, Ila, story time," Gus said, trying to sound cheerful.

Gus lay awake for a long time that night. She could hear Ila across the room, snuffling in her sleep under a pile of bears. She didn't know what time it was, but the moonlight had traveled across the floor and gone, which meant it was very late. She thought about the day, about the swim meet and their mother's increasingly strange behavior. The two things were not connected, of course, but for some reason it felt like they were. She sighed and turned over, trying to get comfortable.

She must have drifted off to sleep, because she was awakened by the creaking of the bedroom door. Footsteps, very light and quick, crossed the floor and stopped by her bed. Gus cracked one eyelid open and saw her mother. She was about to sit up, but some instinct made her close her eye and lie still instead. Her mother put one cool hand on Gus's forehead, as if she were feeling for a fever. Then she traced her thumb over Gus's skin, first in the shape of a cross, and then a circle around that. She did it three times, murmuring something that Gus could not hear. Then she said loudly enough that Gus heard the word clearly, "Shield."

Gus's eyes popped open. "Mom?" she said.

Her mother stepped back quickly. "Oh, Gussy," she said. "I'm sorry I woke you."

"What are you doing?" Gus asked her.

Her mother said lightly, "Just visiting my chicks. Just making sure all is well. Now back to sleep with you." She bent low over Gus and kissed her on her forehead, the same spot where she had been tracing the circle.

Gus wanted to ask her more questions, but her eyelids were flickering and she was too tired to form more words. She drifted back to sleep as her mother slipped out of the room.

In the morning, she remembered her mother coming into her room, but the rest was hazy, and she couldn't be sure she had not dreamed the whole thing.

At breakfast, she said casually to Leo, "Did Mom come into your room last night?"

"I don't know," he said reasonably. "I was asleep. Why?"

"Nothing," Gus said.

Ila looked up from her oatmeal and stared at Gus, the green in her eyes sparking inside the soft brown.

"What?" Gus said, knowing that Ila would not answer her. And she didn't, of course. She just looked at

Gus for another moment and then dug back into her oatmeal.

Gus shrugged and buttered her toast and did not say out loud what she was thinking, which was that her family could really be a bunch of weirdos sometimes.

CHAPTER 3

Eavesdropping

A few days later, when the children got home from school, they were surprised to see their father's car in the driveway. Inside, the house was silent and still. The afternoon sunlight coming through the windows lit up dust in the air. In fact, the whole living room seemed dusty and close, as though no one had cleaned it in months. Gus opened her mouth to call for their father, but Leo stopped her, gesturing up the stairs and holding his finger to his lips. There were voices coming from the second floor, very faintly.

Gus and Leo climbed the stairs together, both skipping the squeaky board on the fourth step. Ila followed them but went into her room to retrieve the bears, who were not allowed to go to school with her.

Gus and Leo went down the long hallway that ended at their mother's studio. The voices were coming from there. The door to the studio hung slightly open in its crooked frame. They could just see their father's back.

He was kneeling on the floor. Their mother was in the rocking chair. Her hands were limp inside their father's larger hands.

"Rosemaris," their father said, sounding weary, as if he'd been speaking for hours. "How can I help you?"

"You can't," their mother replied. She bent her head farther so that her shining hair, as smooth as water, fell over her face. "No one can. I just have to focus. Only I'm not sure I'm strong enough, not after all this time. I don't know how long I can protect them."

Their father gathered her in his arms. She laid her head on his shoulder and closed her eyes.

"I should have known this would happen," she said. "We've been so naive, Peter. What were we thinking?"

"I love you," their father said. "I loved you then, and I love you now."

"I should never have come to you," their mother said. "And now the children are going to pay for my recklessness. I just want—" Her voice broke and she took a shaky breath. "I just want them to have normal lives."

She turned her face into their father's shoulder. Her own shoulders heaved as she wept.

"They will," their father said. "I promise you, they will."

Their mother's reply was muffled.

Gus was suddenly horribly frightened. Without speaking, she and Leo backed away from the door. They got Ila from her room, and the three of them went to the kitchen.

"Pay for what?" Leo said, moving automatically to the cupboard to pull out cookies. "What in the world is she talking about?"

"It doesn't make any sense," Gus said, pouring the milk. "But at least she's talking, right? I mean, she's barely said a word in weeks. Not that there's anything wrong with that," she added quickly.

Ila didn't seem bothered by Gus's comment. She just took a glass of milk with her thank-you smile and then crouched back down on the floor to share it with the bears.

"What does she mean, come to you?" Leo said. "Do you think she means when they met?"

"I don't know," Gus said doubtfully. "She didn't really come to him, right? I mean, she was drowning. That doesn't really count as coming to someone."

"Grown-ups always say weird things," Leo said, but he sounded doubtful too.

Gus took the cookie Leo had been dunking and leaned down to give it to Ila. "Yeah, whatever," she muttered.

That night, before dinner, Gus took a long, hot bubble bath. The bathroom was the only room in the Brennan house with a lock on the door, and for that reason it was Gus's favorite. She locked the door, filled the tub, and floated happily for a while. Then, slowly, she slipped under the water, so that she was totally submerged. Long ago, she had discovered that if she lay underwater in the bath, she could hear her family moving about downstairs through the bottom of the tub. It was very faint, but it always gave her a feeling of safety just to know that they were down there.

Gus let her hair float up around her face and blew some bubbles, feeling sleepy and warm. She should be coming up for air, she knew, but oddly enough, she didn't feel any need to. Then this oddity was eclipsed by another. She realized that if she closed her eyes and concentrated, she could actually hear her mother and father speaking downstairs, probably in the kitchen. That had never happened before. Their voices were as clear as if they were in the room with her.

"Listen to me," her mother was saying. "This is important, Peter. I'm not sure I can do this. I'm not strong enough. You have to take them to her."

"No," her father said sharply. Then, more gently, he added, "Nothing's going to happen. You're imagining things, Rosie. And we agreed that they would never go there. You left all of that behind you."

There was a moment of silence, and then her mother spoke again. "I thought I did," she said, "but now I think that you can't escape your past. I was a fool. And now it's up to us to keep them safe. Promise me, Peter."

Gus strained to hear more, but there was only a long silence, followed by footsteps as someone—she thought it was her father—left the kitchen.

Gus suddenly realized that she was freezing. The

water around her had grown tepid, all the bubbles dissolved. As she had that thought, she also realized that she was still underwater, and that she had not surfaced for air in—how long had it been? Long enough to hear the conversation between her parents. Long enough for the water to grow cold. She burst out of the water in a panic, scrambling over the edge of the tub to lie on the bath mat, gasping and choking.

"Gus, is that you?" she heard her father call. He was standing outside the bathroom door. "Did you go and drown in there?"

No, but I should have, Gus thought wildly. She pinched her arm just to make sure, but she wasn't sure of what. That she wasn't dead? That she wasn't dreaming?

"Gus?" her father said, sounding concerned.

"Um, I'm fine," she said shakily. "I'm OK."

"Well, dinner's ready. You sure you're OK?"

"Yes," she said, thinking, *No, no, no.* "Yes. Dinner. I'll be right there."

She toweled off and put on pajamas, her head still spinning. What had just happened? She needed to talk to Leo.

"Gus!" her father shouted. "Come *on!* We're waiting for you!"

Gus went downstairs. She would talk to Leo about it later. But the conversation at dinner was about the possibility of her getting a puppy for her upcoming birthday, and then there were dishes to clear and stack in the dishwasher and spelling words to practice and she was in bed drifting off to sleep before she remembered it. When she woke up again, it was to the sound of Ila screaming, which shocked the whole incident out of her mind entirely.

CHAPTER 4

The Night Poem

Ila's bed was empty, so Gus followed the sound down the hallway to her parents' room. Ila must have gone in there in the night, because she was sitting up in their bed in her nightie, and although she had stopped screaming, her face was red and she was crying. Their mother was leaning over her and murmuring. Their father stood at the end of the bed in his pajamas.

"Just a nightmare," he said to Gus and to Leo, who had joined them and stood blinking. Leo obviously had fallen asleep while reading in his clothes again. "Everything's OK."

Ila nodded sleepily and snuggled in closer to their mother.

"Tell you what, you two," their mother said. "Come over here to the bed and sit with us for a few minutes."

"Can I get my book?" Leo said.

Their mother patted the bed. "Come on. You don't

need your book. Just for a minute. It will make Ila feel better."

Ila turned her sleepy, tear-stained face to them, and Leo sighed dramatically.

"OK, I guess."

Leo and Gus crossed to the bed and sat down. Ila crawled over to Gus and leaned against her legs. Their father remained standing, now framed in the doorway.

"OK," their mom said. "Instead of a story, I'll tell you a poem. From when I was a little girl."

"When you were little?" Gus said, intrigued. Their mother never talked about her childhood.

"That's right," their mother said. "I don't know why I haven't remembered it before. It's an old, old thing, from way before I was born. Ready?"

She began to speak, slowly at first, as if she were trying to remember the words.

> *On this night,*
> *This darkest hour*
> *This hearth,*
> *This house,*
> *This hold.*
> *On the fire*
> *On the bower*
> *On the young*
> *And old.*

"'On the fire' and 'On the bower,'" Gus said dreamily. "I like that. What's a bower?"

"It's a dwelling," their mother said.

"There's a bowerbird that lives in Australia," Leo said from his side of the bed.

Their mother laughed. "Well, this bower is a dwelling. The poem is an old prayer to protect the home. You say it at night, before you cover the fire at the hearth."

"Who would say it?" Gus asked, trying not to sound too eager. "Your mother?"

Instead of answering, their mother said, "There's another verse. Would you like to hear it?"

"OK," Gus said, feeling slightly defeated.

Their mother leaned over and gave Gus a quick squeeze on her leg. "Right," she said. "Let's see if I can remember the rest."

> From the forest
> From the fen
> From the flame
> And sea,
> Salt and iron
> Rock and den
> To fight
> To shield,
> The three.

A sharp gust of wind buffeted the house. Rain began to slash at the dark windowpanes. Ila whimpered.

Their father had been moving quietly around the room, closing windows. "I'll get the other bedrooms," he said, and disappeared down the hallway.

"Who are the three?" Leo asked.

"Why don't I say it again," their mother said, raising her voice over the sound of the storm, which was now driving at the windows so that they rattled in their frames. "I'll say a line, and you can say it back to me. It'll be fun."

Her voice didn't sound like she was having fun. It sounded thin and tense.

"Again," she said when they had finished, and she started the poem before anyone could object.

Ila huddled closer to Gus as their mother began to say the poem again, stopping at each line so Gus and Leo could repeat it.

Together they recited the poem, almost shouting over the screaming wind, huddled together on the big bed as though it were a lifeboat on a storm-tossed sea. As they reached the last lines a second time, there was a blinding flash of lightning, followed immediately by a crash of thunder that seemed to break right over the house. Ila screamed, and as she did, the lights went out.

Without thinking or pausing, they said the poem a third time, really shouting it now. It was like a game, the poem against the storm, except that there was something frightening about it too. The storm seemed to be fighting their voices, raising its own volume to drown them out.

When their voices died, so too did the storm, dropping away as though it had never been, leaving the room heavy and humid and still. The lamp next to the bed blinked back on. Their father came into the room, lit in the doorway by the reassuring yellow of the hall light, which had also come back on.

"Over already," he said cheerfully.

"Just a squall," their mother murmured. She was lying back against the pillows and looked pale and sick.

"Rosemaris?" their father said, crossing the room to her.

"I'm fine," she whispered. "Just tired. But, Leo, Gus? And Ila too," she added, struggling up to lean on her elbows. She was breathing heavily, as if the motion were almost too much for her. "I want you three to remember that poem, OK? No matter what. It's important to me that you remember it."

"Rosemaris," their father said, a warning in his voice. "You should rest."

"What for?" Leo said. "It's just a poem, right?"

"Of course," their mother said. "Of course it is. It's just a nice thing to remember, that's all. Something from my past that you can keep." She lay back again. "Off you go. It's late. Ila, you can sleep with us tonight."

Gus paused at the door. "What's it called?" she asked.

"What?" her mother said in a distracted voice.

"The poem. What's it called?"

"Oh, I don't know. I always thought of it as the night poem."

"The night poem," said Gus. "I like that."

"Peter, just check outside, would you?" her mother said. She pulled Ila nearer to her and closed her eyes.

"Rosie," their father began, but she spoke again, without opening her eyes.

"Please, Peter. Just, please."

Gus and Leo went to their rooms, and their father headed downstairs. Leo slipped into Gus's room a minute later. Gus was already pulling on a pair of sneakers.

"Let's go," she said. "We'll need to hurry."

Outside, there was no sign of the storm that had passed over them. The moon shone as brightly and cleanly as a white sun, and the stars glittered in a cloudless sky. The moonlight reflected off the ground and cast the backyard in sharp, unfamiliar angles and shadows.

"There's Dad," Leo hissed. Their father was kneeling outside the kitchen window, which meant that he was also under the window to Ila and Gus's bedroom, above the kitchen. He seemed to be looking down at something. He got up quickly when he saw them.

"What are you two doing here?" Their usually easygoing father sounded angry and . . . something else. *Was he afraid?* Gus wondered. The thought made a tingle climb up her spine. "Back in the house," their father said. "Now. I'll be right in."

He walked quickly away from them, to the edge of the yard, where it began to slope down to the rocks. He stood there, turning his head to one side and then the other, searching the darkness. Quickly, Leo dropped to his knees and put one hand, palm down, inside some sort of depression in the soft dirt there. He looked closer. It was an animal's paw print.

"I think it's a wolf print," Leo said. Gus was about to argue, but it *was* much larger than any fox print she had ever seen. It swallowed Leo's spread hand easily. And it was not just one print. The dirt under the kitchen window was crisscrossed with tracks. It looked like several animals had been here, pacing back and forth and then standing in this one spot, where the tracks were deeper.

Gus reached out to the windowsill. Strands of seaweed clung to the edge of the sill where the wood was rough and splintery. "Look at this," she said to Leo. "It's still wet. How in the world did seaweed get up here?"

"Gus and Leo—*now*." Their father was coming back up the yard, and he sounded like he was on the verge of true anger.

"Was it wolves, Dad?" Leo asked.

His father laughed, but his laugh was tight and strained. "Probably a couple of coyotes," he said. "Let's all go to bed, OK?"

They followed their father inside.

Leo paused at his bedroom door.

"Gus," he said, "I saw those tracks in my book. Those aren't coyote tracks. They're wolf tracks. I'm certain of it. There were wolves under that window."

He turned without another word and went into his bedroom. Gus stood for a moment outside Leo's door. Then she went to her room and got back into bed. It was late, or maybe early—it was hard to tell if the gray light was seeping away or growing.

As Gus curled up in the warm hollow under her

covers, she thought about the night poem. Without quite understanding why, she whispered it to herself, from start to finish, just to be sure that she remembered it. It didn't make her feel cozy and sleepy, though. It made her feel afraid. She hoped fervently that when she woke up in the morning, things would have gone back to normal. With that wish whistling in her head like a person alone in a dark room, she fell asleep.

CHAPTER 5

Emergency

The next morning, their mother did not appear, although the children knocked on her bedroom door several times. Leo went to call their dad, who had gone to work as usual. His voice carried up the stairs to where Gus waited outside the closed bedroom door.

"Should we go in?" he was asking. There was a long silence. "OK," he said, and then again, "OK. But come home soon, Dad, please?"

Leo came back upstairs, pushing his glasses up on his nose.

"He said go to school. He's going to come home and stay with her. Where's Ila?"

They opened the door and tiptoed into their parents' bedroom. Their mother was a blurred shape under the covers, her hair as glossy and smooth as a yard of silk across the pillow. Next to their mother, Ila lay curled up. Gus looked at Leo and raised her eyebrows at him. Wake

Ila up or let her stay? Leo nodded and tiptoed back out of the room to call their father again.

"Mom," Gus whispered, thinking, *Please, oh please, open your eyes.* But her mother slept on.

"Mom," she said again, louder. "We need you."

Neither her mother nor Ila stirred at the sound of her voice.

Leo came back. "Dad says to let Ila stay. He's on his way home," he whispered.

Gus nodded. Her last glimpse of Ila and their mother was of the rough red curls of Ila's hair mixed in with the shining black of their mother's, as though they were woven together in sleep, both transfixed under the same unwavering spell.

School that day was a mix of quiet, grim-faced teachers and whispering kids. Max Murphy's dad's lobster boat was missing. Max's dad had been in the boat, along with two other men from the town. They had headed out early Tuesday morning toward the Far Islands, and had not come home for supper. Although no one was saying it, at least not the teachers, everyone knew that the boat was gone, and the men with it.

Max Murphy was in Gus's class, although he was not in school that day. All the kids were talking about it, or passing notes back and forth with guesses about what might have happened, when Max would be back, what it would be like to be sitting at home with your mom and little sister, just waiting. Gus barely noticed. She was so distracted, in fact, that when Emma Flannery, who sat behind her, tried to pass her a note, it just bounced off her leg and onto the floor.

"Gustavia," Mrs. Walker said sharply. "Do you have something to share with the rest of us?"

"What?" Gus said, lifting her head and looking around her.

Mrs. Walker sighed. "Throw it away, please."

Gus got up and threw the crumpled note away without even trying to read it. As she walked slowly back to her desk, she kept her head down and did not look at Emma.

At the end of class, Mrs. Walker asked her to stay behind for a minute.

"Is everything all right, Gus?" her teacher asked, not unkindly. Gus could see that she felt bad for calling her "Gustavia" in front of the class.

"Fine," she muttered. Mrs. Walker waited. Gus wanted to tell her everything—My *mother's sick and my father won't call any doctors and I'm afraid and I'm not old enough for all of this*—but she didn't say anything.

"Are you worried about Max's dad?" Mrs. Walker said.

"What?" Gus said. "Oh, um, yeah. Yes."

Mrs. Walker nodded. "It's a hard thing, I know," she said. "There will be an assembly tomorrow with some more information, and some people will be here if anybody needs to talk more about it."

"I'm fine," Gus said again. "I'm just tired."

Mrs. Walker sighed. "When you're ready to talk,

I'm here," she said. "And don't forget we have our first meeting for the Fall Math Olympics coming up. You're old enough to compete next fall and I want you on the team."

Gus nodded. Last year she had been dying to join the team and travel to Washington, D.C., to compete. This year she couldn't even think about the fall. And anyway, if things had not got better by then, she certainly couldn't leave on a trip. Anything could happen in her absence. She felt heavy with the weight of watching, but it couldn't be helped. Ila was still a baby, and Leo was too flighty. It was up to her, only she didn't know what *it* was, or what she was supposed to do.

"Gus," her teacher said, reaching out to her. "What in the world is going on, child?"

Gus turned and ran out of the classroom.

The hallway was brightly lit and silent. Gus could smell hot food from the lunchroom. She ran down the hallway and up the flight of stairs at the end. Leo's classroom was at the other end of the hall. Running along the corridor, Gus was filled with a certainty that she and Leo needed to get home. They should never have left their mother alone. And what if Ila got hungry and couldn't wake her? Gus was suddenly sure that her mother had not gotten up, not at all, and that Ila was alone and frightened in the house.

She reached Leo's door. Leo was in the G&T class— gifted and talented. As far as Gus could tell, G&T just meant that the kids in Leo's class got to choose what work to do and when to do it, and that no one thought it was weird that Leo split his time between reading about obscure subjects and training two box turtles to perform tricks. Leo even presented his box turtle data to the class, a fact that Gus hoped fervently would never be known by the fifth grade at large.

Looking through the small window in the door to the G&T classroom, Gus could see Leo. He was hunched over a thick book that lay open on his desk. One hand held the pages open while the other wrote furiously in the notebook that he balanced on his lap. Gus watched him, feeling helpless. She couldn't very well knock on the door. It could be hours before Leo looked up.

Suddenly Leo straightened. Turning in his seat, he glanced over to the window in the classroom door. Gus waved frantically at him, and without turning his face away from her, he raised his hand. She couldn't hear what he said, but she saw the teacher nod and then he slipped out of his seat and came to the door. She felt a rush of relief so strong her knees almost buckled.

"We have to go," she told him, and was surprised when he agreed.

"I know," he said. "I felt it too, just this minute. We have to hurry."

Leo seemed to have a plan to get them out of the school, so Gus let him take the lead.

"What was that giant book?" Gus asked him as they moved quickly down the hallway.

"*Physiology of North American Canids*," Leo said absently. "Here." He pushed open the door to the gym and they slipped inside. Their sneakers squeaked as they crossed to the door on the far side. Leo tried it. It was open.

"Mr. Gulden always forgets to lock it," Leo whispered. Once they were on the sidewalk, they ran without speaking. When they reached their house, the last one on a small lane that ended at the ocean, Gus's fear reared up into full-scale panic. There was an ambulance outside their front door. Its red lights were flashing wildly.

"No," Leo said as they ran for the door. Before they could get to it, the door opened and a man came backing out of their house. He was holding one end of a stretcher. They could see their mother's long dark hair hanging off the sides of the white board. From the neck down, she was covered with a blue blanket. Then their father stepped out behind the two men.

"Dad!" Leo screamed just as Gus cried out for their mother. The men carrying the stretcher swept by as Gus tried desperately to catch hold of it.

"Mom," she said, putting out her hands, but the men pushed by her to the waiting ambulance.

"Still nothing. Move it," one of them said, and then, after counting to three, they heaved the stretcher up and into the dark hole of the ambulance and hopped in after it. Gus grabbed for the door. She could see the men working quickly, attaching wires to her mother. One of them put an oxygen mask over her face and the other brought out a box of some sort and paddles.

"Ready?" he asked the other man. Then he turned and saw Gus. "Don't let the kid see this," he said to the second man, who nodded and swung the door closed. Gus could hear them shouting "Let's go, let's go!" as the door slammed shut.

The ambulance siren began, a rising scream that echoed the one rising in Gus's chest. The ambulance pulled away from the curb and raced down the street in a blur of red flashing lights and noise. Gus was left standing with her hands held out in front of her, still reaching for her mother. When she turned back, she saw her father and Leo. They were crouching on the sidewalk with their arms around one another. Leo was crying, but what was more frightening was that their father was crying as well, and Leo was holding him up even as their father held him.

Gus stood still as the red lights disappeared, bearing their mother away from them. All that was left was the siren rising and then falling away, and after that the deep sweeping darkness of silence reaching out for her and pulling her to her knees on the cold concrete of the sidewalk.

CHAPTER 6

Ila Speaks

It was Gus who thought of Ila. As she ran for the house, she saw Mrs. Moore from next door heading for her, but she kept going. The shades in her parents' bedroom were still drawn, but the room was blazing with electric light. Gus could see paper wrappers from medical instruments on the floor, and cast-off tubes and the cap that she guessed went to a syringe. Trying to sound like herself and not some frightened version of Ila's big sister, Gus said Ila's name.

There was no sound in return. Gus turned to leave, but then she heard something, a slight noise from under the bed that made her turn back. She got down on her belly and looked underneath the bed. In the gloom, Ila's eyes shone oddly, as if they were giving off their own light. Ila was scrunched up on the far side from Gus. Ila was not crying but was watching Gus without blinking.

Gus swallowed. "Are you OK, Ila?"

Ila did not answer, of course. But then she crawled out from under the bed, stretched out her arms to Gus, and said, "Moray."

Her sister's speaking voice was tiny but clear, like a small bell being rung very precisely. Gus snatched Ila up in her arms. Staggering a bit under her heavy bulk, she ran down the stairs and into the front hall, where she nearly collided with Leo, who was sitting on the floor.

"Ila talked!" she panted. "Ila said something."

Leo turned his face to Gus. It was streaked with tears and dirt. His eyes were red. "What?" he asked dully.

"Ila. Said. Something," she said slowly. "She said *moray*."

Leo frowned. "What does that mean?"

"I have no idea, but she said it."

Leo put his hand on Ila's head.

"Ila, what's a moray? Do you mean a moray eel?"

"You idiot," Gus said. "Of course she doesn't mean a moray *eel*, do you, Ila?"

Ila shook her head. "Moray," she said again.

Leo jumped to his feet. "I'll go look it up," he said, and ran up the stairs to his gigantic illustrated encyclopedia.

Gus and Ila sat on the floor of the hallway. Ila laid her head on Gus's shoulder. And that was how Mrs. Moore found them when she came into the house to explain that their father had gone to the hospital and that the three of them—Gus, Leo, and Ila—would be staying with her for the next couple of days.

At that, the wonder of Ila's voice was forgotten and the truth crashed back in on them—their mother was lost to them, at least for the moment, and their father may as well have been lost too.

Gus and Ila went upstairs to their room to get pajamas and toothbrushes. Gus stood looking at her unmade bed for a minute, and then before she knew it, she was facedown on it, weeping miserably. Ila came and stood next to her, patting her head with one small hand. Gus didn't hear Leo come in, but she felt his hand on her shoulder.

"I couldn't find any other meaning for *moray*," he said, speaking quickly. "Just, you know, the eel. I mean, I guess we could try other spellings, right . . . ?" His voice trailed off.

Gus turned over and looked at him. He shoved his glasses up higher on his nose, even though they had not slipped down.

"Are we going to be OK?" she asked him.

Leo's hand dropped to his side. "I don't know," he said.

Gus wiped her eyes and kissed the top of Ila's head, and the three of them made their slow way out the front door and over to Mrs. Moore's.

The next morning, Mrs. Moore woke them up with the smell of bacon and eggs cooking. Gus felt stiff and sore, as though she had been hiking all day long the day before. Leo was already at the table with Ila.

"Come on, Ila," he was saying. "Say *Good morning*. Say *Leo*." But Ila only smiled at him and reached for her juice.

Gus slid into a chair next to Leo. Mrs. Moore brought them each a plate piled high with scrambled eggs, bacon, and thick slices of toast with jam. Gus liked butter on her toast. Not that it mattered—her stomach felt far too tight to eat anything anyway.

Leo was shoveling eggs into his mouth. "Thank you, Mrs. Moore," he said as he reached for his toast.

Gus felt a flash of irritation with him. "Can we go to the hospital?" she asked.

"I don't know about that, honey," Mrs. Moore said as she came to sit down with them. "Let me call your dad first and find out what he wants to do."

"It's our mother," Gus said pointedly, and then felt horrible. It wasn't Mrs. Moore's fault.

But Mrs. Moore seemed to understand. She put a hand on Gus's arm and said gently, "I'm sure they will let you see her as soon as possible, sweetie."

Hot tears filled Gus's eyes. She pushed back from the table, muttered a quick "Excuse me," and ran upstairs. Gus never cried in front of other people. Crying made her feel prickly and furious, and the thought of being seen crying was even worse.

A while later there was a knock on the door and Leo came into the bedroom. Gus sat up quickly and rubbed her fists across her eyes.

"Mrs. Moore says we can go to see Mom this afternoon," Leo said.

"I guess we won't have to go to school today," Gus said.

Leo nodded.

"I'm scared," Gus said. Leo crossed the room and sat on the end of the bed. They stayed like that for a long time, neither of them speaking, while the morning sun made its slow way across the unfamiliar rug in the unfamiliar room.

From the outside, the hospital looked like an overlarge house. But the lobby was clearly that of a hospital, with people in wheelchairs and, on one bench, a woman crying quietly on the shoulder of an older woman. Gus started to feel angry, which meant she was going to cry again. Fiercely, she pinched the inside of her arm until the pain chased out the tears. She took a deep breath and followed Leo and Ila and Mrs. Moore into the elevator that would take them to their mother.

Their father met them in the hallway. His face was covered in stubble and his shirt was wrinkled and untucked.

"Fish," he said, using his special nickname for them. The children ran to him, and he knelt down and held them tightly.

"OK," he said finally, straightening up. "Listen to me carefully. Mom is sleeping right now. They've given her medication to keep her that way while they try to figure out what's going on. So that means there are a lot of wires and gadgets and things. But don't be scared, OK? Because she's in there, she's just under a lot of junk." He sounded like he was trying to talk himself into something. "OK?" he said again.

"OK," Gus said.

"They think she can hear you," their father continued. "Well, they don't actually know, but oftentimes people in comas can hear, so don't be afraid to talk to her."

He didn't seem to realize he had said the word *coma*. Leo looked frightened. Their father ran his hand through his hair.

"OK," he said distractedly. "OK, let's go, then." He picked up Ila, who did not protest, and they made their way into the hospital room.

Their mother was a small ripple under the sheet. A tube ran from her nose to a machine next to the bed. More tubes ran from her arm and from under the blankets. They could hear a whooshing noise and, over that, the beeping of machines. *Keeping her alive*, Gus thought suddenly. The machines were keeping her mother alive.

"Mom?" Leo said, and then he and Gus were on their knees next to her. Their father shifted Ila onto one hip and took one of their mother's hands. It lay there, pale and limp in his larger hand.

"The kids are here, Rosie. Gus and Leo and Ila are here." Their mother didn't move.

"Mom," Gus said, and then ran out of words. How could she talk to this sleeping doll? She looked like she should be lying in a glass coffin, waiting for a prince to kiss her and bring her back to life.

"Mom," Leo said, his voice loud in the hushed room. "Mom, Ila said something. She talked to Gus!"

Their mother lay still.

"Ila spoke?" their dad said sharply.

"Yes," Gus said, remembering. "She said *moray*, like the eel or something. It doesn't really make sense, but still—"

Gus was looking at her father when she said this. All of the color had gone out of his face, leaving him as pale as the sheet that covered their mother.

"She said *mórai?*" he whispered.

Gus said, "Dad?" a little frightened now.

Just then, the machines around their mother began frantically beeping, and an alarm like a bell went off somewhere above their heads.

"Rosemaris!" their father cried, and then the room filled with people shouting and pushing.

"Get the dad and kids out of here!" someone said.

"Mom!" Leo shouted, twisting in the hands that held his shoulders. Ila let out a piercing scream as another nurse scooped her up. But their mother had disappeared under a sea of white coats and blue scrub pants. Gus heard someone say "Now!" and then the door slammed shut, leaving them alone in the hallway, clinging to their father.

Something is coming, Gus thought. She could almost see it crouching low just outside her vision. Even as she wept wildly into her father's jacketed shoulder, furious and frightened and full of grief, she could feel it waiting.

CHAPTER 7

Wolves at the Window

They sat for hours in the small room at the end of the hall. Their father bought candy and a crossword book, but no one felt like eating or playing a game. Leo had a book that must have come from one of his pockets, and he was hunched over reading it. Ila drew horses and bears on a large pad of paper and then fell asleep slumped against Gus's shoulder. Gus sat totally still and watched the black hands on the large round clock on the wall tick forward. Inside she was concentrating fiercely, saying over and over to herself, *Live, live, live.* The clock ticked on and on and Gus kept thinking her wish in tune to the dull sound of the hands creeping past each black slash and number. Finally, a doctor appeared in the doorway. She was pretty, with curly hair and green-edged glasses.

"Mr. Brennan?" she said, and their father jumped up. She smiled, looking at Gus and Leo as well, so that they were included in her smile. "Your mom is doing just fine," she said to them, and then nodded to their father to join her in the hallway.

Gus shrugged Ila off her shoulder and the children crept after the doctor and their father. The door was open a crack, and they bent their heads toward the sound of voices in the hallway. Gus could just see the doctor's face. She was not smiling anymore. She looked grave and was speaking urgently to their father.

"Any medication at all?" Gus heard, and then "Waiting on more tests, but I have to say I'm baffled by the—" Leo shifted, and the sound covered the doctor's next few words.

"Shhh!" Gus hissed at him.

"Yes," the doctor was saying. "We got her back this time, but I'm afraid, Mr. Brennan, it doesn't look good. I'm so sorry."

She put one hand on their father's arm as she spoke. He bent his head for a long minute. Then he said, "I don't want the children to see her like this. And I don't want anyone else allowed in. No visitors but me, please."

The doctor nodded. "I understand."

Gus, Leo, and Ila pulled away from the door hurriedly as their father and the doctor shook hands. When he returned to the small room, they were sitting side by side on the couch, waiting for him.

"Well," their father said in a loud, jolly voice. "Mom's resting and everything looks good."

"I want to see her," Gus said.

"Me too," said Leo.

Ila nodded stoutly.

Their father knelt down so that he was looking at the three of them. "Your mom needs to rest," he said. "The doctor has decided that she can't have any visitors for a little while. I can check on her, but that's it. The doctor doesn't want her to be disturbed while she's getting better."

"That's not—" Gus began furiously, but Leo kicked her. "Not fair," she corrected herself. Her father didn't even seem to hear her. He was looking away from both of them, lost in his own thoughts. Then he shrugged his shoulders sharply, as if waking himself up out of a dream.

"Let's go home, my fish," he said, and they stood up because there was nothing else to be done. Their father had never lied to them about anything. He always said that honesty was not just the best policy, but the only one. But he had just looked them in the eyes and lied. Walking down the long, bright hallway with her father and her brother and sister, Gus suddenly felt more alone than she had ever felt in her life.

That night, Gus, Leo, and Ila had supper at Mrs. Moore's house again. They were to stay there while their father slept at the hospital.

"I want to see her," Gus said bitterly to Leo.

They were sitting in what Mrs. Moore called the sun room. It was a small room with a skylight and two wicker couches. The space was filled with plants, which gave it a pleasant, green sort of smell. They had escaped to the sun room after dinner, as soon as they had cleared their dishes. Mrs. Moore had offered them television, and usually they would have jumped at a chance to watch because they did not have a television in their own house, but tonight they wanted to be alone to talk.

"Dad lied," Leo said. "He's just trying to keep us out."

Gus nodded. Ila, watching Gus, nodded too.

"Did you see his face when I said that Ila spoke?" Gus said.

"I looked up *moray* in my encyclopedia," Leo said. "It's also a town in Scotland. Or, rather, a council area. Whatever that is. In the northeast."

"Well, that's incredibly useful," Gus said, covering her fear with sarcasm.

"You don't have to bite my head off," Leo said huffily.

"Watcher," Ila said.

Leo and Gus both sat perfectly still.

"What did you say, Ila?" Gus said quietly.

Ila looked up at her. No one had brushed her hair in days. It was wild and curly, a fiery red cloud around her eyes, which tonight were as green as the midsummer sea, with only a thin circle of brown at their very edges.

"Watcher," she said again.

"What 'watcher,' Ila? Watching who?"

Ila said nothing.

"Please, Ila," Leo pleaded. "Please tell us."

But Ila refused to say anything more.

Leo and Gus talked late into the night, keeping their voices low so they would not wake Ila, who was sleeping on an air mattress between the twin beds. Leo thought they should question their father.

"We need to find out what Ila is talking about," he whispered. "Something's going on here, Gus, and I think she's the key."

"Don't be an idiot, Leo," Gus whispered back. "Ila's not a key! She's our weirdo sister who won't say anything but some word that might mean eel and might mean nothing at all."

Leo looked so hurt that Gus felt bad almost immediately.

"I'm not an idiot!" he said angrily to her. "And something *is* going on, Gus! Why doesn't anyone know what's wrong with Mom? Why won't Dad talk about it to us? What's going on with Ila, who, by the way, is not weird?"

Both of them looked down at Ila. She was sound asleep. All that was visible were her curls, spilling over the pillow.

"I don't know," Gus said miserably. "I don't know anything."

Leo turned over, his back to Gus, and pulled a thick book from under the bed. As Gus fell asleep, she could see Leo, still reading by the light of his bedside lamp.

She woke up to the sound of Ila screaming. She threw back the covers and jumped out of bed. Leo was already on the floor trying to wake Ila, who was sitting up with her eyes shut, her face as red as her hair. As Gus sat down on the floor, she pulled Ila onto her lap and tried to rock her, but the child's body was tense and she arched away from Gus.

"Ila!" Leo shouted. "Ila, we're here. Stop screaming, Ila."

"Wolves," Ila sobbed, burying her head in Gus's shoulder. "Wolves."

"What is it?" Gus asked her.

Ila lifted her head and looked at her sister. "Wolves," she said, and then she started to cry again, letting out great, heaving sobs while Gus and Leo petted and soothed her. Mrs. Moore, who had appeared in a flowered nightgown and fluffy slippers, fluttered around them.

"I told you it was wolves," Leo said to Gus, but she shot him a look to be quiet in front of Mrs. Moore.

They gathered around the kitchen table. Mrs. Moore had made hot chocolate, even though it really was almost summer.

"It will help us all feel better," she promised, and the thick, chocolaty drink *was* making Gus feel less panicked, although she was still shaken. She was used to Ila's silence. This newly speaking Ila was a stranger to her.

Ila sat on Mrs. Moore's lap with a cup of warm chocolate. She looked tired now, holding her cup in two hands but not drinking from it. She yawned and let her head slide onto Mrs. Moore's shoulder. She would not talk again, no matter how much Gus and Leo coaxed her. Finally, they stopped trying and sat in silence as well, sipping their drinks.

*　*　*

The next morning, while Ila was drawing at Mrs. Moore's kitchen table, the twins slipped out and went next door to their own house.

"I checked the wolf book," Leo said over his shoulder to Gus as they walked.

"I figured. What did you find?"

"Well," her brother said grimly, "it sure wasn't coyotes leaving those tracks. Remember the size of them, Gus? Way bigger than my hand."

They were at the house now. They went without speaking to the area under the kitchen window. Gus could see a few green strands of seaweed still clinging to a rough spot on the windowsill. It had not rained since that night, so the tracks would certainly still be there. Only they weren't. The soft dirt under the kitchen window was smooth and blank. There were no prints. But when Gus knelt down, she could see that the dirt *had* been disturbed. There were long furrows cut into the soft surface, as though a rake had been drawn over it.

"Someone wiped them out," Leo said behind her. "And look, Gus." He pointed over her shoulder to the right, where there was another mark in the dirt. This one was a design of some sort, a circle cut into the ground. The lines were sharp and clear, as if someone had dragged a stick through the dirt very carefully and with a lot of pressure. The circle was cut into four sections by a cross. The quartered circle reminded Gus of something, or someone—the memory hovered just outside her reach. Bending down, she put her hand out to touch the strange symbol, but Leo grabbed her sleeve and stopped her.

"Don't," he said. His voice sounded strained. Gus took her hand away reluctantly.

"We need to talk to Dad," Leo said, sounding very unlike the easygoing brother Gus was used to. He sounded angry. "Enough secrets."

Leo pulled Gus to her feet and across the lawn. Gus let herself be pulled, but her head was whirling with the strangeness all around them, and something else. It wasn't possible, couldn't be possible, but just before Leo yanked her hand away from the circle cut into the ground, Gus could have sworn she felt heat rising from it.

CHAPTER 8

The Mórai

That afternoon, when their father walked in the door of Mrs. Moore's house, Leo, Gus, and Ila were waiting for him.

"Ila's been waking up screaming about wolves," Leo said as soon as the door had closed.

"Wolves," Ila agreed, nodding.

"I know," their father said, running one hand through his sandy hair so that it stuck up like Leo's. He didn't even seem to notice that Ila had spoken. "Mrs. Moore and I have been talking about it."

"But what are you *doing* about it?" Gus demanded.

"It's just a nightmare," their father began, but at the stubborn look on Gus's face, he cleared his throat and said, "Tonight, guys, OK? Dinner at home, just us."

So that night they ate supper at their own house, with their father. In the morning he was to return to the hospital, but for one night at least, he was home and they could all sleep in their own beds. Their father ate his dinner distractedly, without looking at his food, so that every few forkfuls came up empty. Their old father would have laughed at himself, wiggled the empty fork, and made a joke about being too busy to watch himself eat. This new father just shook his head and put his fork back down to his food.

When they finished eating, their father pushed his chair back from the table but did not get up. He seemed to be thinking about something. Eventually, he laid both his hands flat on the table. Taking a deep breath, he looked in turn at each of them: Gus, then Leo, and finally Ila.

"I need to talk to you," he said, "and I need you to listen closely."

Gus's stomach began to roll over and she felt as though she might be sick. *Please, not Mom,* she thought. *Please, please.*

"I've made a decision," their father said. Leo nodded. Gus did not. Their father cleared his throat. "That is, your mom and I made a decision. We made it a long time ago. Just in case . . ." His voice trailed off. "Just in case this time came."

"I don't understand," Gus said. "What do you mean, you made this decision a long time ago? Did you know Mom might get sick?" Her voice rose. "Has she been sick all this time, and you didn't tell us?"

Her father reached out and put his hand over hers. "Gussy," he said. "There are some things we haven't told you about your mom's family. About where she comes from."

"She's an orphan," Leo said. "She was drowning and you saved her—"

Their father interrupted. "We haven't told you everything. We—your mom and I—hoped that we would never need to. It's old history, nothing to do with our lives here. It should be behind us." He shook his head like someone with water in their ears after swimming.

"We thought it *was* behind us," he said again. "But it's not. And your mother and I both feel that no matter what, the most important thing is that you three are safe. And yes, we talked about it, before your mom got sick, and"—he stopped and cleared his throat—"and after," he said quietly. "And we agreed that you three must be kept safe, no matter what."

"She wants us to go to someone," Leo blurted out. "A woman, right?"

Their father looked at him, and Leo blushed. "We heard you," he said.

Their father nodded. "Yes. Your grandmother."

"Grandma Brennan's dead," Gus pointed out.

"Your other grandmother. On your mom's side."

"What other grandmother?" Gus and Leo said at the same moment.

"Your Mórai," their father said, and all of the hairs on Gus's arms stood straight up, the way they had once just before lightning struck the chimney of their house.

"That's the word Ila was saying," she said. "Moray."

Their father pulled a pen out of his shirt pocket and wrote it right on the cloth napkin.

"It's spelled M-ó-r-a-í," he said. "It's Irish." He sighed heavily, and placed both palms flat on the tabletop, spreading his fingers wide and studying them. "She lives on one of the Far Islands."

"No one lives on the Far Islands," Leo said promptly.

The Far Islands were islands in the Gulf of Maine, except they weren't, not really. They were just rocky heaps, the tips of undersea mountains that had been covered by the water many thousands of years ago. They were uninhabitable, visited only by seagulls and napping seals.

There were fishermen's stories about the Far Islands, though. It was said that they were wreathed in strange, thick fogs that appeared and disappeared at will. Some of the islands, the fishermen claimed, moved at night and could never be found in the same area twice. And the creatures that had been seen on the islands—seals, but also stranger creatures that walked upright like men. Fishermen fished all around Georges Bank, the deepest part of the Gulf of Maine, but none would go out after dark, even with radar, for fear of running aground on one of the Far Islands.

"Your mother's family lives on one of them, or at least they did," their father said shortly. "Only the Móraí is left now. But it doesn't matter. You're not going there."

"What?" Gus began hotly.

Their father held up one hand for silence. "Your mother's side of the family," he began, and then stopped, took a breath, and began again, awkwardly. "Your mother's people, they're—they're not like other people. They're half wild, I guess you could say, and they're dangerous. I don't want you mixed up with them. I'm going to take you to Pop Brennan's instead. I have to be at the hospital, but you guys can stay with Pop for a little while, until your mom's better and this is all over. It'll be fun."

"But, Dad," Gus said, "I don't want to leave Mom. And why do we have to go anywhere? And what about her family? And what—"

Leo interrupted her. "When do we leave?" he asked.

Their father looked at them with such love and such intensity that even Gus was silenced.

"Now," he said. "We leave now."

Things happened very quickly after that.

"Run upstairs and pack one bag each," their father said. "Just one each—that includes books, Leo. Bring a couple of warm sweaters."

Their father sounded so strange, so frighteningly unfamiliar, that they did not ask any questions. They just went upstairs and packed. Gus went into Leo's room to get her favorite sweatshirt—well, Leo's sweatshirt, really, but after stealing it for more than a year, she considered it hers. Leo was putting his book about wolves into his backpack. Then he pulled another book off his shelf and put it in as well. Gus was able to read the words *Mythical Beasts of the* before he yanked the flap closed, glaring at her.

"Whatever," she said quickly, pretending not to care. "Don't forget to feed Bilbo and Gimli," she added, knowing that would distract Leo.

"The turtles!" Leo said in dismay. Grabbing a notebook, he crouched on the floor to write a lengthy note on turtle feeding and training for their father. While he was writing, Gus was able to grab the sweatshirt from his closet and get it back to her room, where she stuffed it into her pack.

She added an extra sweater to her bag, and a flashlight.

Ila packed her bag full of bears.

"Sorry, Ila," Gus said grimly. "And no time to fight about it either," she added.

Ila sat glumly on the bed while Gus unpacked her backpack and refilled it with clothes. At the top of the bag, she jammed in Ila's favorite bear, the soft brown one with floppy ears. Ila took the backpack huffily and rearranged the bear so that its snout was poking out of the top of the pack, and then followed Gus downstairs, where they found their father waiting in the hallway, holding their water bottles. They each took their own bottle and then stood for a moment, waiting for Leo. He came down the stairs clutching his turtle care instructions, but when he saw the look on their father's face, he simply put the sheet of paper on the hall table and took his water bottle from their father's outstretched hand.

"OK, then, fish, let's swim," their father said, trying to sound jolly and failing miserably. "OK," he said again, more quietly. "Let's go."

* * *

Their grandfather lived inland, in a little town by the border with Canada. They drove north on the coastal highway rather than cutting over, which made Gus glad—this way she could keep the ocean in sight as long as there was light.

The car was quiet. Leo and Ila slept in the backseat, Ila in her booster and Leo with his head mashed into the space between the window and the seat back. Gus didn't sleep. She had so many questions that she had given up even trying to ask them. She felt that she was in some sort of strange dream, where the only option was to follow along. She pressed her forehead against the cool of the window and watched the colors leave the landscape, leaching out as they drove until all she could see was dark shapes that were trees and sleeping houses.

After a while, she turned to watch her father drive. He was wearing a baseball cap with *Eppies* written in curlicue script across the front. He drove intently, with both hands on the steering wheel. They looked strong, the knuckles square and battered from his years of hauling in lobster pots as a young man. She suddenly had a feeling that she was not going to see him for a long time.

"I love you, Dad," she said into the quiet of the car.

"I love you too, Gussy," he said without taking his eyes away from the road.

"What's going on?" she asked him. "I mean, really."

"Not now, OK, honey? I need to focus on getting us there."

"Fine," Gus said shortly. She turned her face back to the window, determined not to speak to him again until he was ready to explain some of this . . . this craziness. It was too much. Gus was angry and frustrated. And she had to admit, she was curious too. Even as she was thinking this, she slid into sleep, an uneasy, shallow sleep populated with wolves and schools of frightened fish and the unending sound of the sea in her ears.

Gus woke with a start. Her father was reaching over her to unhitch her seatbelt. "Let's go, everybody," he said.

"Are we there?" Leo asked sleepily.

"No," their father said as he scooped up Ila, who was clearly unhappy at being uprooted. "We're going to stay here tonight and finish the drive in the morning."

They were in a dirt parking lot. In front of them was a small green building made of wood, with a front porch on which there sat a rocking chair. Behind the little house, in a semicircle set back almost to the woods, sat more cabins, each with a porch light shining into the deep night. A sign on the door said *Ring bell on the right*.

Their father rang the bell, tentatively at first, and then with more force. After some time, a woman came to the door. Her face, which was pinched with sleep and irritation at being awakened, softened when she saw Mr. Brennan with Ila sleeping in his arms.

"Late night for such little ones," she said sympathetically. "Well, come on in and I'll get you a key."

They followed her into the small office. Something moved in the corner and a large black dog unfolded itself from a blanket on the floor. It came to Gus and pressed its nose into the backs of her legs. She patted its head absently while she leaned her other arm on the counter. The dog took a long, luxurious sniff, and then suddenly his whole body stiffened and he backed away from Gus, growling.

"What is it?" Gus said, reaching her hand out to the dog. He crouched against the far wall, alternately growling and barking, his hackles raised all along his back.

"It's OK, boy," Leo said, stepping toward the dog. The dog crouched and whined in fear and then began barking again, high and shrill and sharp.

"Charlie!" the woman shouted. "Charlie!" But the panicked dog ignored her.

"Stay back, Gus," their father said. "You too, Leo. Give him space."

The woman came around the counter and dragged the still-barking dog outside by his collar, shutting the door behind her. She was back a minute later.

"Well, goodness me," she said to Gus. "Whatever did you do to that dog?"

"I didn't do anything," Gus said indignantly.

"I'm just teasing you, love," the woman said. "But honest to God, I haven't seen him like that in fifteen years. I didn't know he could still bark. Must have something on your clothes, I guess."

Gus's father shot her a look that said *Behave*.

"Fine," she muttered. "But I didn't do anything."

"One night, please," their father said. "We'll pay cash." In the ledger, he wrote the name *Will James* in a strong, round hand totally unlike his usual scrawl.

"OK, Mr. James," the woman said. "You can have cabin eight. It's just out back of here—pull right up to the door."

"Thank you," he said. "It has been a long day."

He sounded totally normal—not like someone who had just signed a fake name on a ledger at a motel in the middle of nowhere, Gus thought sourly. They followed him to the car, pulled out their backpacks, and stumbled into cabin eight.

Their father carried Ila into the tiny bedroom where the three children would sleep. The cabin smelled like wet swimsuits left too long in a bag. Gus and Leo sat yawning on the couch, which was covered in a hairy plaid material. Their father came back out.

"Off to bed," he said. "You can sleep in your clothes. We'll get an early start."

As she slid between the chilly sheets, Gus could see their father through the half-open bedroom door, standing in the hallway. Guarding them, she thought.

"Gus," Leo whispered. "How late do you think it is?"

"I don't know. Past midnight?"

"But it only takes two hours to get to Pop's. If it's past midnight, we've been driving for at least four hours."

Gus tried to answer Leo but found that she was just too tired. Instead, she breathed in the air from the open window, cool and faintly tinged with the smell of salt and something else, something green and sharp. *Maybe seaweed*, she thought sleepily. And then, taking one more deep breath of the lovely sea air, and with all of her questions still circling around in her brain, she fell fast asleep.

When Gus woke up again, the bedroom door was closed. The only light in the room was coming from a small night-light plugged into the wall. And there in the dim glow, next to her bed, was a creature, something like a large brown weasel.

The creature was sitting up on its haunches, and it was speaking to her.

CHAPTER 9

A Night Visitor

I'm dreaming, I'm dreaming, I'm dreaming, Gus thought frantically. The weasel, or whatever it was, twitched its large, bushy tail in what was clearly impatience. It was far too big to be a weasel, she realized. Standing on its hindquarters, it was almost as tall as Ila. Its thick, reddish fur smelled like that of a wet dog, one that had taken a good long roll in rotten seaweed.

"Come, come," the creature said. "Get up, stupid little girl."

Gus had opened her mouth to scream, but when the creature called her *stupid,* the insult wiped out her fear. Gus was very sensitive about her brain, as anyone would be with Leo for a brother. "I'm in eighth-grade math," she whispered furiously.

Leo interrupted whatever the creature might have said by waking up and saying very quietly, "Gus. Shut up." Then, speaking even more quietly, he said, "That's a mink. Don't move, Gus. Just stay still. It's probably rabid—"

The creature turned and said crankily, "I am most certainly *not* rabid. What is it with you two? We do not have a lot of time, you know, and this is not easy for me either. And for your information, I am not a mink. I am"—and here the creature stretched itself up proudly to its full length, swishing its furry tail from side to side as a balancing aid—"a sea mink."

"Extinct," Leo sad flatly. "Eighteen ninety-four."

The creature dropped down on all fours and looked balefully at Leo. It had small, rounded ears, which it pinned back in a very clear show of displeasure. "Do I look extinct to you?" it demanded.

"For goodness' sake," Gus burst in. "It doesn't matter! I mean, whatever-it-is is talking, Leo! I don't think—"

"The last sighting of a sea mink was in 1894, in New Brunswick," Leo said desperately. His face was very pale, and he looked at Gus, not at the creature, who was beginning, very slowly, to arch its back.

It stretched and hissed, and then, quite suddenly, standing in front of them was a small, elegant-looking man in a dark overcoat. He yawned and gave a little bow, smiling at the children, who sat with their mouths hanging open.

"The Bedell," he said, and bowed, a very deep and formal sort of bow. "At your service."

As he straightened back up, Gus turned on her bedside lamp and took a longer look at him. He was small, not much taller than Leo, and enveloped in a long coat that reached all the way to the ground. He was wearing woolly gloves with the fingertips cut off. His fingernails were long and curved over themselves. They seemed to glow with a faint pink light, like the insides of oyster shells. His face was smooth and unwrinkled, with high cheekbones and large, dark eyes.

"You must be Leomaris, and you are Gustavia," he said, shaking their hands in turn. The parts of his fingers that were not covered by the gloves felt freezing and slightly damp, as if he had been washing in cold water just before he arrived. He spoke with a very slight accent—French, Gus thought, but not quite. He sounded a bit like the lobstermen from Nova Scotia who sometimes came to Maine in the winter to sell their hauls. His speech, however, was far more precise and formal than the Canadian lobstermen's.

"And my, oh my," the man said, turning to Ila, who was wide awake and sitting up. "Just look at you, little one." She smiled up at him, and then slipped off her cot and crossed the room to climb into bed with Gus. Sitting there with the warm weight of Ila against her, Gus decided not to be afraid.

"Mr. Bedell," Leo asked, his voice quavering slightly. Leo clearly had not reached the same conclusion as Gus about the little man. "Um, not to be rude, but were you just an *animal*? And why are you . . . what . . ." He stopped, clearly frustrated, and, leaning over, he picked up his glasses from the bed stand and shoved them on his face. "Why are you here?" he said more steadily.

"I am here for you, of course!" he said. "I am taking you to Loup Marin."

The twins looked at each other. "Loup Marin?" Leo asked.

"Well, of course," the Bedell said impatiently. "Where the Móraí waits for you. She is the Watcher there," he added helpfully.

The children stared at him in silence.

"You are Folk," he said. "Your mother is Folk, and so you three are as well. It is time for you to come home."

"Folk?" Gus said. "What in the world is that?"

"*Who* is that," the man corrected her. "You and the boy are approaching the doubled year. Your power, therefore, is growing."

"The doubled year?" Leo said.

The Bedell looked at the three of them again and sighed like an exasperated teacher with very slow students. "Anyway, here I am, and here we are, and so on, so forth, etc., etc., and we must get a move on, yes?"

"We can't just go off with a . . ." Gus couldn't think of what to call this strange visitor, so she dropped it. "We can't just *go*," she said lamely.

The man looked at her, and all the jolliness was gone from his face. "There is very little time," he said. "The wolves are on the trail. Your father did well to drive you in circles all night—he almost lost me, and that is saying a lot. But if I can find you, the wolves can too. With your mother ill— Oh yes," he said, noticing Gus's startled expression, "I know all about your mother. Anyway, she has done as much as she can do. The only thing left to do is run."

"What if we don't?" Leo asked. He wasn't being belligerent. Leo never held grudges, and anyway, he looked more fascinated than annoyed now by their odd visitor. He was just being Leo, and that meant gathering all the facts that were there to be gathered. "What if we stay here, and go to Pop's tomorrow with our father?"

"I doubt very much you will ever arrive," the Bedell said, his nose twitching in an agitated sort of way. "The King's wolves will find you, just as sure as a flounder is flat."

One foot (bare, and covered in fine brown hair) jerked in the air as though trying to find something to scratch.

"This is America," Leo said. "We don't have kings."

"And this is Maine," Gus added. "We don't have wolves, especially not wolves who go around *killing* people!"

"Your mother will certainly die as well," the little man continued, as if neither of them had spoken. "She has used up all her strength trying to hide the three of you."

At the man's words, an image of their mother swept over Gus, one of her before the illness, laughing at the dinner table at one of her father's silly jokes—*Where does the king keep his armies? In his sleevies!* She suddenly missed her mother, needed her, more than she could stand.

"Don't you talk about our mother," she said angrily. Ila whimpered as Gus tightened her arms around her.

The little man stood with his hands held loosely

together in front of the lapels of his coat, the way a squirrel sitting on its haunches holds its paws, looking at Leo and then to Gus and Ila and back to Leo again.

"Who is this 'king' person anyway?" Leo said.

"Has no one told you anything?" the man said impatiently. They all shook their heads. "Yes," he said, "I am afraid that your father—"

And with that, the door burst open and their father came in, his hair in wild disarray, his face tight with fear.

"What is it?" he said sharply. Then, as he took in the three of them sitting up on the beds, his shoulders sagged and he heaved a sigh of relief. "What are you guys doing up?" he said in a quieter voice.

Barely daring to breathe, Gus peeked over toward the Bedell. The floor was bare, save for a small puddle of water where the man had been standing. Gus could smell a faint odor of wet dog and seaweed coming from under her bed. Pushing Ila off her lap, she swung her feet over the edge of the bed.

"Um, Dad—" Leo began, but Gus cut him off.

"Sorry, Dad," she said. "We're just worried, you know, about stuff."

Her father's face softened. "I know, Gussy," he said. "But you need your sleep, OK?"

He came over to the bed and scooped up Ila. While he tucked her into her cot, Gus swung her feet energetically. They hit something soft and furry and, still thinking about her mother, she kicked backward as hard as she could. There was a muffled squeak from under the bed.

Their father sat on Gus's bed, and then gathered her up in his large embrace. His sweater smelled like cold night air and the piney aftershave that their mother gave him every Christmas. Gus buried her head in her father's shoulder and breathed in the smell of him. Finally, he let her go and stood up.

"We are going to be fine," he said. "Gus? Leo? We are going to be fine." He bent down and kissed the top of Leo's head.

Gus noticed that he didn't say that their mother was going to be fine. In a flash, she knew that everything the small man had told them was true. They were in terrible danger, and their mother was dying. Staying was only going to make things worse, possibly much worse.

"OK," she told her father, and while it wasn't quite a lie, it felt like one.

Their father paused in the doorway. The light from the hallway lit him from behind, so that she couldn't see his face. *I need to see it one more time*, she thought wildly to herself, but her father just said, "Love you, fish," and eased the door closed.

After a minute, the strange creature—the sea mink—crawled out from under Gus's bed. He dug in his claws and stretched his body out to an impossible length, and then, with a ripple that ran from his nose to the tip of his long tail, he changed into the Bedell, standing in the middle of the room in his heavy overcoat.

"Not a very sweet girly, are you?" he said bitterly to Gus, fingering a fresh bruise under one eye.

"You were nasty," Gus told him. "There's no reason to be mean."

"Why didn't you let me tell Dad?" Leo asked Gus.

"Because Dad won't tell us what's going on. Don't you want to know?"

"I guess," Leo said doubtfully. "I mean, yes. I do."

Gus fixed the small man with her fiercest look. "So tell us. What's going on?"

"You must come with me now," the man said softly. "There is terrible evil rising in the sea. Your mother knows, and your father knows as well, although I do not know if he truly believes it. Surely you have noticed something amiss."

"The missing boats," Gus said. "And the high tides?"

"But I thought the tides were from global warming," Leo said. "That's what Dad said. The sea level is rising from the melting at the polar ice caps."

The man shook his head. "That is happening, yes. But the things that are happening here, the tides and the missing boats, are not human problems, I'm afraid. The Mórai will tell you more. But there is very little time. Morning is too late. We must go now."

"Yes," Ila said.

"OK, Gus?" Leo said.

Gus was remembering her father's warning about their mother's family. But what choice did they have? Hiding at Pop Brennan's was clearly not going to change anything, and might even put Pop in danger. She looked at Leo.

"Dad" was all she said, but she knew her twin would understand.

"You said Dad won't tell us anything," Leo pointed out. "And he wants us to go to Pop's, which is starting to sound like a really bad idea."

"Wolves," the Bedell reminded them. "They would of course kill anyone they found when they arrived," he added.

"Not Pop!" Ila said. Ila adored Pop Brennan. He had never tried to trick her into speaking, seeming to prefer sitting in silence next to his youngest granddaughter. He also never brushed her hair, something that went far with Ila.

Slowly, Gus nodded. "OK, I guess," she said. She felt something in the pit of her stomach at the thought of deceiving their father. Not guilt, exactly. It was something sharper than guilt. A feeling like she was breaking something that existed between them, changing their relationship forever. It was just fear, she decided, giving herself a shake. But the look on her twin's face told her otherwise. He felt it too. They were stepping out of their lives into something completely unknown. And their parents could not be a part of it.

Ila, sitting next to Gus on the bed, suddenly shifted and took Gus's hand. Ila's hand was small and slightly sweaty. Gus gave it a squeeze and Ila squeezed back. Leo sat down on the other side of Gus, leaning his shoulder into hers, warm and solid. Sitting between her brother and sister, Gus felt some of that terrible feeling slide away.

"Wonderful," the Bedell said. He clapped his hands together, the sound muffled by the woolly gloves that he was wearing. His strange, curved fingernails flashed in the light. "Without delay, then."

"What about a note?" Leo said. "Shouldn't we leave a note?"

"No need."

"Well, I'm writing a note," Gus said defiantly. She jumped off the bed and fished around in the bedside table's drawer. She found a small black Bible with a fake leather cover and a ballpoint pen. Under the Bible was a pad of paper with the words *Maine: The Pine Tree State* printed across the top of each page. She tore off a sheet and wrote quickly, without thinking about how crazy it might sound. *"Dear Dad, we are going with Bedel–"*

"Two *l*'s, if you don't mind," the creature said. "It is the French word for *messenger*."

"Does he even know who you are?" Gus asked the man.

"Most likely, no," the Bedell admitted. "But that is no excuse for a lack of precision. Two *l*'s, if you please."

Gus sighed and added another *l*. *"We are going with Bedell to Loup Marin Island."*

"Actually, it is *the* Bedell," the man said. "More of a title, you know, than an actual name."

Gus gave him a dark look.

"But write what you will," he added hastily.

"Bedell," Gus wrote, leaving out the *the* with a small sense of triumph, *"says we will be safe there. Do not worry*

about us. We will be home—" She paused again. "When will we be home?" she demanded.

The man shrugged.

Gus stared hard at him.

"Just say *soon*. Will that do?"

"Fine," Gus said primly. She finished the note and signed it, *"Your children, Gus, Leo, and Ila."*

"No more lollygagging about," the man said. "We must move, move, move."

Ila hopped off the bed. "Let's go, then," she said gravely, and the Bedell, taking her hand, made a little half bow toward her.

"To the sea," he said. Looking at Gus and Leo, he said again, "To the sea. And then we *travel*."

CHAPTER 10

Traveling by Sea

They followed Bedell, or *the* Bedell, as he insisted on being called, out of the bedroom and through the dark living room, sliding their feet cautiously along. Their backpacks were dark lumps by the front door. They picked them up without speaking and put them on, Leo helping Ila with her straps.

The four small windowpanes in the front door were flat black squares, but when they followed the Bedell outside, they could see gray at the edges of the night—it was not far from dawn. The Bedell led them around to the back of the cabin and across a wide, mowed lawn. The lawn dropped away at its edge to rocks. They could hear, but not see, the waves below them. They sounded far away.

"Go down on your bellies, yes?" the Bedell whispered. He himself merely crouched low to the ground and picked his way down the rocks as though they were a set of stairs.

Gus and Leo put Ila between them. Ila did not hesitate but instead began scrambling so quickly that Gus and Leo had to struggle to keep up with her.

"Just because she can see in the dark," Leo grumbled. "Ow!" He stopped and rubbed his knee where he had banged it on a rock.

Ila laughed. Her voice carried on the still night air.

"Hush," the Bedell hissed. He climbed back up to where the children were. "Come, come," he said urgently.

They slid down the final series of rock ledges, landing on soft sand. The air around them was lightening with morning, and they could see that the beach was actually low, sloping rocks, black and shiny with seawater. Beyond the rocks was a horseshoe-shaped patch of sand, just large enough for the four of them to stand huddled together.

"The sea," Ila said.

"That's right, little red hair. Off we go," the Bedell said. He smiled then, his teeth gleaming. They were small and sharp-looking, coming to points at their ends. He had the same glossy hair and round brown eyes as their mother, but the Bedell seemed wilder than their smiling mother. When the Bedell smiled, he looked hungry.

The Bedell rubbed his hands together as though trying to warm them. "There is no real time, see, no time, that is, uh, for what you might call, ahem, *formalities*. Give me your backpacks."

"Why?" Ila said. She clutched her backpack and looked at the man suspiciously.

"To keep them safe," he said. "Now give them to me, please."

Gus saw the look on Ila's face, and the way the green sunbursts in her eyes began to spark with a dangerous light. "Bear will be fine," she said quickly. "It's OK, Ila. See?" She handed her own backpack to the Bedell, followed by Leo.

The Bedell nodded his thanks and then held out one gloved hand to Ila. "Come, child," he said, his voice quite gentle now.

Ila snuck a quick kiss onto Bear's head, which Leo and Gus politely pretended not to see, and then handed over her pack.

The Bedell took Gus's backpack and put a strap into one of the pockets sewn in the side of his coat. The strap filled the pocket entirely. But as they watched, he tucked the entire backpack into the pocket, bit by bit, like a magician tucking a handkerchief into his closed fist. When the pocket had swallowed the last of it, he put Leo's backpack into the same pocket.

"Now yours," he said to Ila. "I will put it in a special pocket." He tucked Bear's head into a chest pocket in the coat, sewn over the place where his heart beat. Bear's head disappeared into the small pocket, followed by the rest of the backpack.

The children stared openmouthed. What they had just seen was not possible. The coat hung smooth against the Bedell's body, with no trace anywhere of the three backpacks.

"How did you—" Leo began, but the little man, waving his hands in a dismissive way, interrupted him.

"You two," he said to Gus and Leo. "Have you passed your birthday yet?"

"Our birthday?" Gus said. She found that she was whispering too. "Why?"

"Your eleventh birthday, I am correct?" The little man said. "Have you passed it, yes or no?"

"Uh, no," Leo said. "Not for a few days."

"So," the little man said. "Not so good. But it is OK. I can help you. I will have to Turn the little one anyway, so I will just Turn all three of you, yes?"

"Turn?" Leo said.

The Bedell nodded. "Do not be scared. There is really no choice—we must heffely-lump back to the island or we will not get there at all! Now take hands, you three."

The three children joined hands and stood in a ragged line in front of the man, who opened the lapels of his long coat like a peddler about to show off watches and gadgets. But instead of trinkets, there was only darkness. It was unlike the darkness of night or of a closed-up room. It was somehow gleaming, as though it had been taken out and polished like a gem and then replaced. The children stared transfixed at the luminosity rolling out from between the little man's wide-open arms. It danced and swirled like a field of oil on fire.

"Listen to the sea," the Bedell called, which was easy enough—the sound of the waves crashing seemed to be growing louder by the minute. "Tip back your face to the spray and then breathe, breathe, breathe!"

Gus could feel Leo's and Ila's hands gripping hers, but she could see nothing, and hear nothing but the rushing of wind and water in her ears. She felt the sensation of someone or something *pulling* on her, turning her inside out. She felt sick and, falling, pitched forward as if in a dream when your body plunges into bottomless darkness. She cried out for Leo and threw her arms out to break her fall. From far away she heard Leo call her name and the sound of Ila laughing. She tried to shout for Leo again, but the rushing was too great—it filled her ears, her eyes, her lungs, until she was in the black itself, splintering to glittered fragments—then with a thump, she landed on solid ground.

She stayed like that for a few seconds, breathing. Then she lifted her head and saw in front of her two creatures. One was the sea mink, standing sleek and low to the ground. The other, a rounder creature, balanced on the rocky ground. It was larger than the sea mink, and while most of its coat was gray marked with darker spots, its belly was a creamy white. The animal's face was the same flecked gray as its body, with big, dark eyes set far apart above its rounded muzzle and black-button nose.

It was a seal.

Gus blinked to clear her vision, but the slightly blurred images did not shift. She also noticed that the sea had gone from blue to black, and the morning sky above it was a steely shade of gray. She put her hands up to rub her eyes and fell forward heavily with a surprised noise that sounded like the hoarse bark of a dog. Instead of hands, she had two flippers. She was balanced awkwardly on the front of her body, pushing herself up with the flippers so that she could lift her head and look around.

"No time to sit here and think," the sea mink said sharply.

The other seal's long white whiskers quivered. Its brown eyes darted around wildly.

Gus squeaked. She could barely breathe. What was happening? And why did the seal in front of her look so familiar?

The Bedell solved the mystery for her. "Leo!" he growled to the other seal. "Stop gawking. If you want to survive this trip, you must move."

Suddenly from behind the sea mink stepped a very small, very beautiful fox with a white-tipped tail and four white paws. Although it too looked gray, Gus could tell from the way light came off its coat that it was a vivid color, and most likely a red fox.

The fox grinned, showing very white and pointed teeth.

Gus's head was spinning. The sleek fur was standing up all along her back. She and Leo were *seals*? And this *fox* was her baby sister?

"Oh no, this will not do," the sea mink said in his

hissy voice. "How on earth did you manage that? Well, it is not safe to travel in that form, little one. No, no, no. Come now, the sea, please."

The little fox stamped the ground with a paw.

"This is a bit of a disaster," the sea mink said to no one in particular. "Very strong child. Naughty, strong child."

He turned back to the little fox, who watched him with her tongue hanging out in a foxy grin.

"Ila, my dear," he said in a syrupy, wheedling voice.

Leo snorted.

"Ila, won't you please think of the sea now, just give it a little thought, the fish and the water, and the lovely, dark deeps . . ."

Gus felt her skin prickle at the man's words. She found she could barely stay on the beach. The sea was so near, and it smelled so *good*.

The fox, however, made a sound somewhere between a yowl and a human laugh, and trotted past the mink and directly into the water, pausing to splash playfully in the shallows.

The sea mink arched his back and hissed, showing his sharp little teeth.

Gus could smell the fear on him. There was no mistaking it—a tang like rust on iron. In fact, she realized, she could smell *everything*. She sniffed the scent of salt and, under that, the nervous brine of swimming fish, which made her nose twitch uncontrollably. She smelled the green bite of the stubby trees that clung to the rocks above the beach, and the damp, charcoal smell of the granite. And under that, approaching on the breeze, a familiar smell of soap and piney aftershave. Then the smell of salt and brine and the sweet flesh of clams and the ticklish smell of sardines and the heavier, meaty smell of something larger swimming out in the deep drove the familiar scent out of Gus's nose.

She found that by humping her back up and pushing off with her front flippers, she could move over the sand. Leo struggled along beside her.

At the water's edge, Gus stopped. She had a sudden feeling that if she went into the water she would never come out again. The Gus that she knew herself to be would be lost forever. She couldn't move. Leo, beside her, hesitated as well. The smell of pine aftershave grew stronger, pulling her back.

Then, hearing a familiar voice, they turned. What they saw, blurry and black-and-white, but clear enough not to be mistaken for anyone else, was their father. He was scrambling down the steep rocks, slipping and falling and rising again, shouting his children's names.

"Ila has gone," the sea mink said. "She will drown on her own."

Indeed the small fox was now swimming, her tail waving like a slight flag above the black Atlantic.

"Gus! Leo!" their father shouted.

"You must stay with her," the Bedell said. "Or lose her forever."

And so the two seals slid into the water.

Their father reached the beach and fell to his knees with his hands stretched out in front of him, as if he could somehow pull them back.

Gus and Leo hung uncertainly in the water for a long moment, watching their father. Then the salt-scented sea called them in and down, and they scooped in lungfuls of air and dove.

CHAPTER 11

The Skidbladnin

They dove deep and then straightened out. It was glorious. For as long as she could remember, Gus had been having the same dream. In it she was using her entire body to move through the water, her arms stretched out behind her and her legs kicking together like a mermaid's tail. The water did not seem to have a temperature—it was just a clear substance that held her as she arched her back slightly for power and glided forward. And now, immersed in the Atlantic, she realized that what she had been dreaming of all these years was this—inhabiting a body that was made to move through liquid with so little effort that it felt like flying.

Leo nudged her and she turned in the water to look at him. Although it was dark, the darkness seemed no impediment to sight. The delight in Leo's eyes was clear. He rolled once, twice, then bumped Gus with his nose, urging her. She tucked her chin slightly, pushed through the water with one flipper, and rolled, over and over next to

Leo, spinning faster and faster until her dizziness made her stop and hang in the dark water next to him.

They could hear their own heartbeats, as well as each other's. On land, Gus's heart had been racing. But as soon as she was underwater, her heart had slowed down so much that she could scarcely keep track of its beats. The deep thud, counterpointed by Leo's, soothed her, like a familiar song sung very slowly and softly.

Then there was another, quicker sound that grew into a series of trills and whistles, and a school of silvery salmon rushed by, their small hearts pittering in their bodies. The whistling noise was the water passing through their gills. Leo laughed in delight, although it came out as more of a honk. They could *feel* the salmon hurrying by—their whiskers picked up the vibrations of the passing bodies.

Gus could just see Ila's four legs churning above her head. She popped up effortlessly to the surface to take a breath and to check on the small fox. Leo popped up next to her with a loud *huf*. Ila was swimming easily, her muzzle tipped up against the salt spray of the water. The morning air was crisp and delicious, but both Leo and Gus were eager to go back under.

The Bedell was waiting for them under the surface. It was clear that his fear had disappeared. Whatever threat had been hounding him had withdrawn. He seemed to feel at home here, zipping up to the surface for a breath and then barrel-rolling in the lighter-colored water before diving down again to where the seals swam.

They continued forward in an easy silence, Ila on the surface, Gus and Leo below, and the Bedell moving between them like a flashing ribbon of shadow, here and then gone. As they swam, the sun rose and traveled through the sky, warming the upper layers of the water.

A school of flat, light-colored fish with downturned mouths swam past. *Stripers,* Gus thought with a sudden surge of hunger. The fish, as if sensing her regard, flicked their tails and dove as one, down into a deep gulch cut into darker reaches of the sea. Leo looked at Gus. Gus and Leo had known each other for every moment of their lives, even the nine months beyond memory, and they often could tell what the other was thinking without exchanging words. And now Leo was thinking one word: *chase.* Gus bobbed her head, and then the two seals dove and leveled out behind the fleeing stripers, knowing the stripers were quicker but chasing anyway for the sheer joy of using these new bodies.

After a while, they grew tired and began to look around for the Bedell and the little red fox. When they popped up, the weather had changed. The water was churning, as though spun by a giant invisible hand. Clouds blocked the sun, and rain hissed and spat on the surface of the ocean. Peering about them, the seals saw waves being whipped into tall peaks, and in the middle of the tallest of the peaks, struggling to stay afloat, was the little fox.

"Ila!" Gus shouted to her, but her barking cry was caught by the wind and carried off, effortlessly. It was possible that Ila could hear nothing at all now except the scream of the wind, the guttural calling of the heavy waves, and her own frantically pounding heart.

For Gus and Leo, the sudden roiling anger of the ocean meant little—they could simply dive to where the water was still. Or they could ride the waves on their sleek bellies, letting the water break over them. It was nothing to their noses and eyes, which they could seal against the water, and their lungs, which kept them from needing air for ages. But this was not the case for Ila.

Ila was frightened and growing tired. A wave slapped at her and spun her around. She sank under its insistence before popping back up, lashing out in all directions with her strong legs, her eyes rolling in panic.

Gus and Leo swam under Ila, trying to boost her up onto Leo's back. The little fox was far too frightened to understand what they were doing, and she scratched frantically, sliding and kicking and gulping seawater.

Then the Bedell surfaced next to Gus. Without any warning at all, he Turned and was a man, struggling to stay afloat. His black overcoat was pulling him under, yet he made no move to take it off.

"Your seal form would have served you better, young one!" he shouted.

Treading the water with one hand, he held the other hand out in front of him. There was something resting in his palm. He called out in a language that sounded a little like French but broader, full of long vowels and strange consonants. Suddenly he was blown backward as the tiny thing in his hand leapt up and unfurled, crashing into the water as a raft with one sail and a sturdy-looking, flat-planked floor.

Leo understood immediately, and with one powerful heave, he shoved the drowning fox up onto the edge of the small boat, where she scrabbled for her footing and then gained the raft and stood, her sides heaving and seawater running off her body. The boat seemed unmoved by the rolling sea, sitting lightly on top of the water like a toy boat in a bathtub. The fox sank to her belly, exhausted and trembling.

Without a word, the Bedell, who was a sea mink again, set off. The boat followed obediently in his wake, as though he were pulling it, but they could see nothing connecting the two.

Gus and Leo followed on the surface, both keeping an anxious eye on the fox, who slept as though enchanted. The boat rode easily over every cresting wave, and its deck and the small body curled up there remained as dry as an August afternoon.

Gradually, the water beneath them began to brighten. A sudden flash of silver streamed under them—hundreds of tiny fish dodging the seals with one swift dip. They began to smell, very faintly, mussels, and sweet crabs hustling away from them. This time, they ignored temptation and kept their eyes focused on the boat carrying their sister.

After a long while, they sighted a small island that was alone in the water. Dodging underwater shoals, the seals swam through the light froth to where the last of the waves slapped at a rocky beach. Leo hauled his unfamiliar bulk onto the black rocks, Gus just behind him. The little boat, which had been waiting for them in the shallows, bumped up on the rocks as well. Ila woke up and, hopping into the shallow water, dashed forward onto the rocky beach. She shook herself, looking delighted all over again.

The boat continued forward, propelled onto the beach by an invisible power, its deck dry and unmarked by either salt or water. Then the Bedell stood there in his black overcoat. The boat folded itself into a small box. The Bedell put the box in a small leather pouch, and closing his fingers around the bag, he slipped it into one of his pockets like a bit of sea glass. He looked at Gus and Leo, who were still seals, and said shortly, "Skidbladnin. Gnome-made boat. I, ah, removed it from some rather sturdy warrior types some time ago, but water under the bridge, let us hope!"

With that, he stretched his hands out to both of them, and they each felt a strange pulling on their seal coats, as if two hands were smoothing them from nose to tail. The smoothing accelerated into tugging, and then, with a sudden hard yank, they were pulled up and dumped back down on the sand on their human backsides, in soaking wet human clothing. Leo's glasses hung crookedly from one ear. Color rushed in so abruptly it felt like noise—the hot orange of the lowering sun, the navy sky, and the brilliant red coat of the little fox who sat in the sand with her tongue out, grinning.

Gus squeezed her eyes shut in pain. When she opened them again, the Bedell was just closing the two wings of his overcoat.

He spread his arms out wide and smiled his fierce little grin at them.

"Welcome to Loup Marin," he said.

CHAPTER 12

Loup Marin Island

Gus and Leo remained sitting on the cool sand of the little beach. Gus's head was spinning, and she thought she might be sick. She also felt a sharp stab of disappointment, almost a pain, and she could tell from Leo's face that he did too. It was like taking off a lovely costume and putting on your bland old street clothes again.

Ila, however, was still a fox.

The Bedell stretched out one arm and spread the fingers of his hand. His intent was clear—it was a gesture of power and command.

"Yes," he said sharply, and the red fox's coat began to shimmer, as if in a heavy wind. She reared up and stamped the ground with her front paws, for all the world like a human child having a tantrum.

Then the fox turned to run.

The Bedell lifted his other hand and brought it level with the first one. Ila reared up one more time and then fell forward into her human body, landing on the beach on her hands and knees.

She jumped up and stood with her chubby fists on her hips, scowling furiously.

The Bedell bent forward and put his hands on his knees. He stood that way, breathing heavily, for a moment. Then he straightened up.

"We must move on," he said.

Gus looked up at the little man. She felt too exhausted to stand.

"What happened?" she managed to say. She meant all of it, but the Bedell misunderstood.

"You are just lucky I was there," he said irritably. "Otherwise, she would have drowned for certain."

"Thanks for warning us," Gus said angrily.

Leo, sitting next to her, put a hand on her arm. "It's OK," he said. "We're OK. But, um, Bedell, what just happened? How—"

"Come now, children," the Bedell said, and his voice was softer, gentle even. "I am afraid you cannot wait any longer. Time is moving all around us. We must step into it."

He reached into one of his overcoat pockets and pulled and tugged and pulled again until Gus's backpack popped out. Next came Leo's, and finally Ila's, with Bear peering out of the top of the pack. Ila yanked Bear out and gave him a quick, fierce squeeze. Leo looked anxiously inside his backpack—checking his books, Gus guessed. With a light sigh, he tightened the flap back down and hoisted the pack.

The Bedell set off without a word, leading them across the small beach. They scrambled over a long stepped shelf made of granite. Above the shelf lay more rocks leading upward, mixed with small, scruffy pine trees with twisted trunks and low bushes that clung to the bits of dirt between the boulders.

They stood for a minute, looking up. Loup Marin was a pile of boulders. Above was only rock and pine, with no visible path through them.

"We're going up there?" Gus said skeptically.

"Just a skip and a jump," the Bedell said. "Follow me. Stay close. Mind your feet."

With that, he began to climb, twisting his way among the boulders as though there was a path. And in fact there *was* a path. It was very faint, but the children could just see where many feet over time had flattened the dirt or a boulder had been moved to allow passage. The island, which appeared to be an uninhabitable pile of rocks, was definitely inhabited, or at least it had been at some point.

Ila, scrambling over a boulder, suddenly cried out.

Gus turned back quickly, but it was just Bear, who had slipped from Ila's hands and was wedged in a deep crack. Gus fished him out by one strap of his overalls.

"Into your backpack," she said sternly to Ila.

"Sorry, Gus," Ila said in a small voice.

Leo grinned. "At least she's talking. That's good, right?"

"Good, good," the Bedell said. "Now hurry up and mind your hands and feet. This last part is a bit tricksy."

They scrambled up the steep section, Gus in front and Leo boosting Ila when she needed it. As they reached the top, the Bedell put out a gloved hand and pulled each of them up and over the lip of the granite. They stood in a loose semicircle, breathing hard from the climb.

The Bedell swept one arm out in a dramatic gesture. "Voilà."

"Wow," Leo said.

They were standing at the top of the island. Instead of gray rock, a meadow stretched before them. It was wild-looking, made up of tough stalks and low bushes that would be full of blueberries later in the summer. Right now the color came from the green grass and tiny pale pink, lavender, and white bell-shaped flowers. Far off to their right and left, they could just see the ocean. The fog had lifted and the water spread out, deep blue flecked with sparkles and the white crests of waves. Gus turned slowly, taking in the view. It was the most beautiful place she had ever seen.

"Not long," the Bedell said over his shoulder, moving at a brisk trot. "Watch your step," he added just as Gus tripped on something hidden in the grass. It was a rough pile of rounded stones, tumbled as though they had once been part of a wall, or a gate, or—

"A house," Leo said, crouching down. "It's an old foundation of a house. Here's where the doorway was."

Gus could see the break in the stones. It did indeed look like it might have been a doorway, and now that she was looking closer, she could see the depression in the grass that must have been the foundation.

"It was tiny," she said.

"Come now," the Bedell said impatiently.

Gus rose to her feet. "Did people live here once?"

"A long, long time ago," the Bedell said. "Long forgotten. Now it is just the Móraí. And me, of course."

"Do you live here too?" Gus said, surprised. The dapper little man did not seem to fit this wild island.

"Indeed," he said, and began walking again.

The children followed the Bedell over the hilltop meadow. As they reached the far edge, it dropped off into granite again, shielding its lush secret from any passing ship. At the very edge of the stony cliffs, a house sat waiting for them.

Except that it was not a house at all. It was a lighthouse.

"Cool," Leo said approvingly.

The structure rose tall and white from the rock's edge, seeming to hang over the ocean below. There was no grass anywhere around it. The gray of the rocks was broken here and there by green and yellow mosses.

As they drew closer, the children could see that there was a very small, white-painted cottage with a dull red roof crouching in the shadow of the lighthouse, hidden from the sea.

The cottage and the lighthouse were bordered by an iron railing built in a semicircle on the ocean side of the buildings. Beneath the railing, the rocks dropped sharply into the Atlantic, which hissed and spat against them.

"Very cool," Leo said again, and Gus had to agree, although it did look a bit lonely, with only seabirds and crashing waves for company.

The Bedell led them to a door that was almost too small for an adult to fit through. It was the brilliant blue of old dinghies, the paint flaking and peeling off from the salt of the ocean wind. As they drew near, they could see that it had an image painted on it, a fish in vivid silver and gold. Each bright scale on the fish was carefully outlined, and its silver eyes glowed with a fierce and particular intelligence. Gus reached out her hand toward the fish to follow the curve of its leaping body with her fingers. As her fingers made contact with the fish, it shivered.

Startled, Gus dropped her hand.

"Don't touch that," the Bedell said. Reaching past her, he pushed the door open, carefully avoiding the fish, whose painted face now bore a pained expression. The three children went in, Leo ducking his head slightly to pass through the small doorway.

They were in a living room. It was yellow and warm, lit, even in the daylight, by lamps. A blue velvet couch covered with bright throw pillows faced a fireplace and, next to that, a tall bookshelf. Books alternated with other treasures: large and small shells, piles of green and blue sea glass, dried starfish, and odd pieces of driftwood. In a corner of the room, a woman was sitting in an armchair that was turned sideways for a view of the ocean through the window.

She was very small, with snow-white hair woven into a heavy braid that hung over one shoulder. She wore blue jeans rolled several times at their cuffs, a fuzzy pullover, and woolen socks. Her feet did not quite reach the ground.

"Here they are," the Bedell said, presenting the three children with a low bow. Then, turning to the children, he said, "The Móraí."

The woman turned in the chair. Her eyes were brown, set into a wrinkled face that was tanned and creased by sun and water. She looked like an older version of their mother.

"About the little one . . . ," the Bedell said.

"Not now, my friend." The Móraí did not look at him. "Let me see my grandchildren first."

The man nodded and said, "Of course, of course," as he stepped back into the shadows at the edge of the room.

"Now come here," the Móraí said, not getting to her feet.

* * *

The children stood shyly around her until she reached out her arms and gathered them up. Then it was as if a dam were breaking, and exhausted, hungry, and overwhelmed, they all cried a little bit, even Leo, and then they sat on the floor near her and Gus and Leo told her the whole story, starting and stopping and helping each other along and circling back as they remembered other bits and pieces, like the prints under Ila's window, their mother's illness, the way their father had rushed them out of the house. They stopped there, by some sort of unspoken agreement. The trip to the island, the *swim* to the island, was too strange, too unbelievable, to talk about just yet. They sat in silence for a moment, and then Leo said, "Our mother's very sick. She's—" His voice choked off and he stopped talking, taking a deep breath. "She's very sick," he finished miserably. "And we don't know what to do."

"I know all about that," the old woman said. "And I know how frightened you must be, and how worried. But the most important thing, the only thing that matters, is that you are here, and you are safe."

Gus swallowed hard. The past few weeks had been full of such sadness and confusion that she had forgotten what it was like to feel safe.

"Thank you," she said.

The Mórai nodded to her, her face very gentle. Then she looked over Gus's shoulder. "Shall we have some supper, my Bedell?" she said to the darkness by the door.

"Why don't you show the children where they can wash up and then we can all sit down."

The shadows shifted, and the little man stepped out. "Right this way," he said, smiling at the children.

"How long have you lived here?" Gus asked the Bedell as they took turns washing their hands at a low sink. The sink was in its own room. The toilet was in an adjoining room that was no bigger than a closet. It was an old-fashioned toilet with a tall back and a chain to pull on in order to flush. Leo was in the toilet room while the girls were crowded at the sink.

"Since I was quite young," the man said. "Yes, step on that," he added, showing Ila a pedal on the floor. She stepped on it, and water gurgled out of the single faucet.

"It's cold!" Ila said. "You go, Gus." She stepped aside to let Gus wash her hands but insisted on working the pedal herself.

"But you weren't born here?" Gus asked, gasping a little as the icy water splashed over her fingers.

"No, no," the man said. "My kind came from farther north. A long, long time ago."

"Is it true, what Leo said?" Gus asked. "Ila, stop pumping! That's plenty of water. I mean," she added as Ila reluctantly took her foot off the pedal and stepped away from the sink, "I mean, about your kind—the sea minks—being extinct?"

Just then, Leo came out of the toilet room.

"Let me do the pedal!" Ila said, shoving Gus.

"Cut it out, Ila," Gus said as Leo asked, "What pedal?" and Ila started stomping. In the ensuing splashing and shouting and more shouting and apologizing, the Bedell slipped out of the room, and Gus's question was forgotten.

They finally made it to the table, all three damp and hungry and irritable. The Bedell sat at one end of the table, and the Móraí at the other.

"Go on," Leo said to Ila as they slid into the three empty seats. "Tell them you're sorry you flooded the bathroom."

Ila stared at her plate and said nothing. Her face was as red as her hair.

"When I first came here," the Bedell said, "I tried to fill the bathroom with water so I could swim in it!"

Ila looked up and the little man winked at her. "That, my dear, was a flood. It was quite glorious."

Ila grinned at him.

"Now let's eat," the Móraí said.

They ate a delicious dinner of fish and dark greens that tasted of the sea and thick slices of brown bread spread with butter and honey. The three children were ravenous. They kept eating and the Móraí kept refilling their plates until, finally, Leo sat back with a sigh.

"Full," he announced.

"More bread, please," Ila said quickly, as though she were afraid that Leo might ruin it for everybody. The Móraí handed her another slice.

"Are you really the lighthouse keeper?" Leo asked.

The Móraí nodded.

"What—" Gus began just as Leo said, "Um, about that trip here?" but the Mórai cut them off.

"No questions," she said. "Not tonight. We can talk about it all in the morning. You are far too tired tonight to understand any of it."

And indeed, even as she spoke, the children felt a great quiet sweep over them, and with it a yawning exhaustion. The bread slipped from Ila's fingers as she slumped forward in her chair.

The Mórai stood. "I have to smoor the fire. Then we can go to bed."

"What does that mean?" Gus asked sleepily.

"It's something I must do each night," the Mórai explained. "Bedell, please clear up while I show the children."

"You will show them the song of protection?" the little man asked. His voice was wistful.

"Can't Bedell come?" Gus asked.

The Mórai shook her head. "The Bedell can keep an eye on Ila."

"But of course," the Bedell said. "I will watch the child. This is a very good plan." And he busied himself stacking bowls, all the while watching Ila, who slept soundly in her seat.

Gus and Leo followed the Mórai to the living room.

The old woman knelt by the fireplace. Gus got close to see what she was doing. Some distant memory was flickering in her mind, but she could not quite catch hold of it.

The fire had died down to embers. Moving swiftly,

the Morái took a small metal shovel from next to the fireplace and pushed the embers off to one side. Then she smoothed out the ashes and made a flat bed of them. Using the shovel again, she arranged the embers in a circle divided into four parts, cut in the shape of a cross.

"That looks like the mark in the dirt under the window," Leo whispered in Gus's ear.

Gus thought briefly about that mark. Their father must have made it, which meant that he did know something of the Folk, even if he did not approve of them.

The Morái stretched her hands out over the circle cut in four and began to speak.

> On this night,
> This darkest hour
> This hearth,
> This house,
> This hold.
> On the fire
> On the bower
> On the young
> And old.

"It's the night poem!" Gus said joyfully. For a moment, she could hear her mother's voice speaking the words, telling them it was a poem from her childhood, something they said at night before bed.

The Morái stopped reciting the poem. "What did you say?" she said sharply.

"The night poem," Gus explained. "That's what Mom

called it. She told it to us just before . . ." She stopped, unable to say the words.

"Before she got really sick," Leo said, finishing for her.

"So that is what she used," the Móraí said wonderingly. "She remembered it."

"Is it a spell?" Leo asked.

"It's a song of protection," the Móraí said. Her eyes shone brightly, as if she might cry. "It's how this island is protected. Your mother must have used it to protect you. But to use it by herself, and so far from here . . ." Her voice trailed off. "It must have cost her dearly."

"It did," Gus said.

The Móraí finished the poem, the words washing over Gus and Leo like a lullaby.

Then she stood up and said briskly, "Time for bed. Follow me."

Stumbling with exhaustion, Leo and Gus followed the Móraí. In the dining room, the Bedell picked up Ila and followed them to the girls' room. There he deposited her on one of the beds and then took Leo to his room.

Both of the beds in the girls' room had red flannel nightgowns folded neatly on them. Gus changed and crawled into bed. The Móraí was putting the other nightie on the still-sleeping Ila. Through the open door, Gus saw a low, sleek creature, the sea mink, slipping down the dimly lit hallway.

"Thank you," Leo's voice came sleepily from the darkness. The mink paused and dipped its head once, and then was gone. Gus closed her eyes. The last thing she was aware of was the Móraí bending over her to stroke her forehead.

"Safe now, Rosemaris," she whispered.

Gus wanted to remind her that she was Rosemaris's daughter, not Rosemaris, but sleep pulled her down before she could form the words.

CHAPTER 13

The Folk

The next morning when Gus woke up, Ila was already gone from the little room. Gus wandered down the short hallway into the small kitchen, which was painted the same bright blue as the front door. Morning sunshine was pouring in through a window high above the sink. The table, which was covered in red oilcloth with tiny blue flowers printed on it, was set with blue glass plates and white bowls. The juice glasses were the same blue as the plates, but the mugs were made of rough clay, each one painted a different color. A vase of the same rough clay held a spray of yellow flowers. It was an altogether cheerful and welcoming scene, and Gus felt her heart lighten as she pulled up a chair next to her brother, who was already eating breakfast along with Ila.

And the breakfast! Heaps of smoked salmon; rich hot cocoa and tiny glasses of some sort of juice that was as fine and sweet as nectar; small silver eggcups holding eggs perfectly cooked for dipping the fingers of toast in; more of the dark, spicy honey from the night before; and jar upon jar of jam of all different flavors. There was also porridge in the ceramic bowls, mixed with tiny blueberries and dollops of thick cream and the honey.

Leo was creating a tall stack of some sort of soft cheese, salmon, and pieces of brown bread that he then somehow managed to cram into his mouth in one giant bite. "Um," he said happily.

Gus took a sip of the thick hot chocolate. Overcoming her normal aversion to jam on toast, she tried smearing a purple one over a thick layer of butter. It was sweet and delicious, tasting exactly like the August blueberries that they always picked back at home.

As soon as she finished the toast, the Bedell appeared from the kitchen bearing a silver rack of more, hot and buttered. He did not sit down to eat with them but hovered in the background, refilling mugs and fetching porridge for Ila, who gobbled up her first bowl and asked for another.

"Do you want a bite?" she added as he brought her a second bowl. The Bedell smiled his fierce little grin at her.

"Seabirds are more my thing, love," he explained.

It was still a shock to hear Ila's voice. Gus was not sure she would ever get used to it. But she liked it. In fact, sitting at the table with her brother and sister in the sunny kitchen, she felt a surge of optimism. Surely everything would be all right now. Ila was talking, and their mother would be better soon. Things were turning around. She spooned the last bit of egg from her eggcup, which was shaped like a leaping fish whose open mouth held the egg aloft.

The Mórai sat with them while they ate. She did not eat either, but rather sipped a mug of dark, fishy-smelling tea. Gus supposed they should call her *Grandmother*, but somehow it didn't feel right. The Bedell had introduced her as *the Mórai*, and the strange word seemed to fit her.

Surprisingly, it was Ila who spoke up first.

"Who are the Folk?" she asked.

The Mórai nodded. "Yes," she said. "The Folk live in the borders. Sea and land, forest and fen. And always, human and animal."

"The borders between sea and land," Leo said. "You mean the seals, right? What Gus and I were." He blushed as he spoke. It sounded so crazy. Catching his eye, Gus nodded at him, a quick, short nod, just to let him know that he wasn't crazy—that they *had* been seals in the ocean.

"Yes," the Mórai said. "What you were."

"But Ila," Leo said. "Ila was a fox. How did that happen?"

"It was a bit naughty of you, now wasn't it?" the Mórai said, smiling at Ila.

Ila put on her stubborn look. "I liked it," she said.

The Mórai laughed. "You are a sharp little one."

Ila peered suspiciously at her and then, seeing that she was not in trouble, smiled back. "I liked it a lot."

"There are different kinds of Folk," the Mórai explained. "We are the creatures that live in the borders. The thing we all have in common is our human aspect.

Usually we are only the two things—human and animal. But occasionally one of us will carry within him- or herself several aspects. It's rare, but it happens. That's what you are, little one," she said to Ila. "Something special indeed, I think."

"Special," Ila said happily. She dug her spoon into her bowl, whispering to herself, "Special, special, special."

"Yup," Leo said, grinning. "Ila's special, all right." He made quotation marks in the air around the word *special*.

Ila stuck her tongue out at him.

"And you are Folk as well?" Gus asked, looking to the Bedell, who stood behind her.

"I gave the Bedell the power to Turn, but he is not Folk," the Mórai said sternly. Then, softening her tone, she added, "But he has been a faithful servant to the Folk for many, many years."

Gus felt awkward for the little man. She was sorry she had said anything.

"What does *Loup Marin* mean?" she asked, to change the subject. "*Marin* is *sea*, right?"

"*Les Loups Marin*," the Mórai said absently. "*Wolves of the sea*. It's the old name for the seals."

"*Les Loups Marin*," Gus said, liking the sound of the words.

"Anyway," the Mórai added, briskly now, "where were we? The Sea Folk. We gather in the old places. We are in many of the old stories as well."

"Selkies," Leo said. "But selkies aren't real."

"What makes you say that?" the Mórai asked.

Leo opened his mouth and closed it again, shaking his head.

"We were once better known," the Mórai said. "But in time, the division between our world and the human world has widened. The Sea Folk have chosen, more and more, not to be seen. Most of them retreated to their animal forms long ago. For many years, I thought that I was the only one of my kind left. But now you three have arrived."

"Why are you here?" Leo asked.

Instead of answering Leo's question, the Mórai said, "Your mother was to take my place when I was gone, as the next Watcher. It's a hard life here, and a lonely one. I think I did not realize just how lonely it might be for a young girl. I was the Watcher, but I did not watch her carefully enough. One day, while she was out swimming in the sea, she caught sight of a young man fishing. She fell in love with him. She turned her back on this island, on me, on the Folk, on her life. She turned her back and went with him to live in the human world."

"And they got married," Leo said.

"No," Gus said. It couldn't be true.

"Yes. And she had three children," the Mórai said quietly. "Two with the dark hair of the seals and one with the red hair of the foxes."

"Were you mad at her?" Ila asked.

The Mórai smiled. "I was sad," she said, and it was clear from her voice that she would not say more on that subject.

It was suddenly all too much for Gus. "I don't . . . ," she began, but then fell silent. What she meant to say was *I don't like this* or *I'm afraid,* but it all sounded too silly. So instead she just said unhappily, "I don't understand."

"Your mother left the Folk behind her when she married your father," the Mórai explained. "She chose a life on land. And I think she believed that her choice would make you three creatures of the land only. But it does not work that way. The Folk blood is strong, and it came down in all three of you. Had anything unusual been happening to either of you?" she added, looking at Gus and Leo.

"Leo won this swim meet," Gus said. "Remember, Leo? That was weird. I mean," she added quickly, "not weird that you won—"

"I don't, usually," Leo said cheerfully. "Gus is way faster than me."

"But that wasn't the weird part," Gus persisted.

"I swam it underwater," Leo explained. "It was a hundred-meter free, and I just . . . won. I didn't even need to take a breath."

"It was totally weird," Gus said.

"And you?" the Mórai said.

"I don't think so," Gus said slowly. But then she remembered the bathtub, lying under the water listening to her family move around downstairs. She decided not to mention it. It seemed embarrassing, like she'd been eavesdropping on them or something.

"The dog at the motel," she said instead. "He was afraid of me."

Leo nodded. "Me too."

"Was he afraid of Ila?" the Móraí asked.

The twins thought, but couldn't remember. "She was asleep," Gus said. "Dad was holding her. Anyway, the dog was freaked out by *something*."

The Móraí nodded. "As your Folk attributes began to surface, you caught the attention of something very dangerous."

"The King that the Bedell was talking about?" Gus said.

"Yes. The Dobhar-chú."

"The what?" Leo and Gus said together. Ila said nothing. She was watching the Móraí very closely, the starbursts in her eyes gleaming with a steady light.

"The King of the Black Lakes. Or, the Water Hound, although you would never call him that and live."

"A hound?" Gus said in disbelief. "A little dog?"

"Not at all," the Móraí replied. "The Dobhar-chú is something different altogether. Have you never heard of him in tales?"

The three Brennan children shook their heads.

"And Leo's read just about everything," Gus said. "If he was in the stories, Leo would know."

Leo nodded modestly. "Nope," he said. "Never heard of him."

"He is an ancient creature," the Móraí said. "He can breathe in the water, and he can tunnel through rock.

But he cannot live on land. His mother was a wolfhound, but his father was one of the Femori. Do you know who they are?"

"Irish water creatures?" Leo asked, scrunching up his forehead. "I can't quite remember the rest."

"They are very old Celtic demigods. Very unpleasant. Their name means something like *under-demons*."

"Ugh," Gus said.

The Mórai nodded. "They dwell in the darkest parts of the sea, and call down storms and floods and disease on any humans unlucky enough to displease them."

"And one of them is the father of this Dobhar-chú creature?" Gus said.

"Yes. He killed his own mother, and then went to the lakes, where he hid in the deepest of them. Fishermen learned to leave their small ones at home when they took to the water. For many years, he ruled as the King of the Black Lakes."

"King of the Black Lakes," Leo said dreamily. "He sounds like a good villain."

"A very *bad* villain," the Bedell said sharply from the corner of the room where he stood listening. "I will take my leave, unless you have further need of me?"

The Mórai smiled at the Bedell. "Go, my friend," she said.

The Bedell bowed briefly and left the room. They could hear the front door close behind him.

"He has strong feelings about the King of the Black Lakes," the Mórai explained. "The Dobhar-chú offered the sea minks much power if they would follow him. The Bedell alone chose not to fight alongside the King of the Black Lakes. He came to me instead. And when the battle was over and the Dobhar-chú was defeated, the surviving sea minks were without protection. They were hunted down by men for their fur until they were all gone. Only the Bedell remains. But he has paid a high price for his loyalty to the Folk. He is terribly alone in this world."

There was a small silence at the table. No one would say it, of course, but the Móraí appeared to be every bit as alone as the Bedell, both of them marooned on this mysterious island.

Why, she's not our grandmother at all, Gus thought as a shiver ran down the back of her neck like a thread of cold water. *She's much, much older than that.*

"Um, actually," Leo said, interrupting Gus's thought, "I have this book about the proof behind mythical creatures? There's lots of evidence that the gryphon, for example—" He pushed his glasses up, getting excited.

"Stop," Gus ordered him. "I want to hear the rest of the story."

"Fine," Leo said. "Forget it, then." He looked sadly down at his toast.

"Where was I?" the Móraí said.

"The Dobhar-chú," Leo said. "In the lakes."

"Oh yes. The Dobhar-chú. So the creature grew, in both power and greed. He took to the sea, and he amassed an army of creatures to fight for him. A great battle followed between the creatures of the deep and the Folk. The battle was for the entire sea, and all that dwelt in it."

"I've never read anything about Sea Folk and a battle," Leo said.

Gus punched his arm.

"What?" Leo said. "I just said I've never read anything about a battle between—"

"Leo, stop talking," Gus said sternly.

"Sorry," Leo murmured. "It's just—"

"*Leo!*" Gus hissed.

"Sorry," he said. "Go ahead. Please."

"Yes," the Móraí continued. "The battle was a costly one. Many, many Folk died, as well as many of the creatures who had allied themselves with the Folk. The Folk were unable to fully defeat the Dobhar-chú, but they managed to imprison him on an island."

"Why didn't they kill him?" Leo asked.

The old woman started to speak and then stopped and shook her head. "I think that is enough to take in this morning."

"That's it?" Gus said. "You're not going to tell us anything else? I want to know what's going on."

She looked at her brother and sister for support. Ila was peering into her bowl to see if she could scrape up any more porridge. Leo was munching toast.

"Hello!" Gus said angrily. "Ila? Leo? Don't you want to know what's going on here?"

"Well, she just said she can't tell us yet," Leo said reasonably. "Sorry, I'm not sure what to call you."

"*Mórai* is fine," the woman said, smiling at him.

Ila said, "May I have more porridge, please?"

"Come *on!*" Gus said in frustration. "I want to know what happened out there! And I want to know why we're here. And I want—I want—" She stopped herself before she could say *I want my mom*. She couldn't stop the tears that welled up in her eyes, though. "I want to know what's going on," she said instead.

The Mórai nodded. "I know," she said, and Gus could tell that the Mórai meant that she knew what Gus had stopped herself from saying. "Please trust me," she added. "I will tell you everything when the time is right. Why don't you explore the island today? I'll pack you a lunch and you can stay out all day."

The Mórai wrapped sandwiches in cloth and put them in a bag along with glass bottles of water and some delicious-looking cookies and sent the children outside to explore. She was going to the lighthouse to polish the huge lamps at the top, which made Leo pause longingly for a moment. It was clear that he was dying to get into the lighthouse.

"Tomorrow," the Mórai promised him. So Leo put on his sneakers and took the lunch bag and joined Ila and Gus.

"Only stay away from the rocks below the lighthouse,"

the Mórai warned them. "They are slippery and treacherous. Head off to the right and you will see a path down."

They followed a thin track that wove between the boulders, working its twisting way to the sea. The sun shone on the waves and threw off green shots of light that made the children shade their eyes with their hands. The rocky beach gleamed wetly, marked here and there with tide pools.

They went straight to the pools, poking the reluctant sea stars with sticks to watch them curl their arms into their bodies for protection and stirring up the bottoms to flush out the hidden hermit crabs. In one of the pools, Gus and Ila found bits of soft-edged green and blue glass.

Gus's mood gradually lightened. It was a beautiful day, and hadn't the Mórai told them that their mother would be fine? Actually, she couldn't remember if those had been the old woman's exact words, but she thought it was close enough. She helped Ila stuff her pockets full of tiny pink shells. They would all be broken by bedtime, but Ila seemed pleased anyway.

At lunchtime, they found a dry spot high up on the rocks and spread out their picnic. The smells of salt and sea and the tang of fish were so strong that Gus couldn't help drawing in deep lungfuls of sharp, delicious air. The wind flicked her hair against her face. She thought she had never felt more alive than at that moment, sitting there with the sun and wind and the fine salt spray of the sea. Leo sighed happily.

"It's amazing," he said.

Gus laughed out loud.

"But, Gus," Leo said, "did it really happen? Did we dream it?"

He didn't need to say what *it* was. Gus closed her eyes for a minute, remembering the smells and the sounds of the living sea, the power of her seal body moving through the silken water. "We did not."

"But," Leo said, "it's not possible, Gus. We—you and I—we turned into seals? And Ila was a fox? How could it have happened? Maybe the Bedell put a spell on us. Maybe we only *think* we remember, but really we dreamed it. There just isn't any other way."

Gus looked at her twin. It couldn't be true, and yet she wanted more than anything else in the world for it to be so. Because if what the Mórai had told them was true, then it just might happen again. And Gus would give anything to feel it again, to swim without even thinking about it, to turn as if freed from gravity in the lit water, to be *of* the world instead of just in it, to hear fish jumping and smell a mussel cracked open on the beach. She longed for it.

"Really, Gus," Leo said again. He shoved his hair back on his forehead impatiently.

"But I remember it," Ila said.

Leo's face brightened. "The way the sea smelled—"

"Yes," Gus interrupted him. "And remember how we could hear everything, and the way we could spin around and that tunnel of rock we went through—"

"Four legs!" Ila said. "Four legs, and fish!"

"The way the fish ran from us!" Gus said.

And then they were all speaking at once, all three of them, the joy filling them: "And the sunlight—remember the sunlight under the water"—"On the water!" Ila cried—"And remember we could smell the island before we saw it, and the swimming, we were so *fast*, it was so amazing, amazing!"

They finally ran out of things to say.

"I wasn't sure—" Gus began, just as Leo said, "I'm so glad," and Ila said simply, "Again!"

Then they all laughed. It was real. It had happened. And it might, just might, happen again.

CHAPTER 14

Exploring the Island

The rest of the day passed quickly. Gus, Leo, and Ila explored the beach and splashed in the shallow, freezing water until the sun streaked the edge of the sky red. At dinner, they were so tired and hungry that even Gus did not ask the Móraí any more questions.

Leo spent their second morning on the island in the lighthouse with the Móraí, polishing brass bits, winding clockworks, and trimming the wicks for the lantern that warned ships away from the dangerous shoals that surrounded the island.

"It's called a Fresnel lens," he told his sisters. Gus and Ila had wandered into the lighthouse after a morning of shell collecting. Leo was giving them a tour of the lantern room, where the beehive-shaped glass light was kept. "Isn't it beautiful?"

"It doesn't look like a lens," Gus said skeptically.

Ila tapped on the glass. Leo frowned and pulled her

hand back. As soon as Leo turned away, Ila patted spiteful handprints everywhere that she could reach.

The lens, which was enclosed in a giant lantern housing, was easily twice or even three times as tall as Leo. The lantern had glass fins all around it, jutting out like the slats of mini blinds over a window. Leo explained that the fins were actually concentric rings of prisms.

"They bend the light," he explained, "in order to focus it all into a really narrow, really powerful beam. And the lens is shaped like a magnifying glass to make it even brighter."

Gus yawned. Ila surreptitiously patted another section with her sticky hands.

"It was invented in 1823 by a French physicist named Augustin Fresnel," Leo said, somewhat desperately.

"I'm hungry," Ila said.

They left Leo with his lens. "What are all these little handprints?" they heard him say as Gus hurried Ila out of the lantern room and down the narrow stairs to the watch room. Gus liked this room better. It was cozy, with a rag rug on the floor and a rocking chair pulled close to the little round window. There was also a narrow bed covered in a blue blanket and a table with two white-painted chairs. The Móraí sat in one of the chairs. On the table was a tray bearing cups of tea and freshly baked scones wrapped in napkins.

"Why don't you two take your tea and scones to the rocks and eat in the sun," the Móraí suggested, her eyes twinkling. Upstairs, Leo's voice was rising as he discovered the extent of his little sister's handiwork on the glass housing of his beloved Fresnel lens.

They hurried out with their treats while the Mórai carried the tray upstairs. "He won't mind, really," she said as she started up the stairs. "He likes cleaning the glass."

Ila looked disappointed.

As they left the little house, a shadow detached itself from the lee of a large gray rock and slid after them.

"Bedell!" Ila said happily, waving at the animal, who, with a shrug, turned into the Messenger. He smiled down at Ila.

"Cannot sneak around this one," he said approvingly.

Ila reached for the man's hand. They hiked up to the meadow and then settled on a large flat rock in the sun for their picnic.

Leo found them just as they were finishing the scones.

Ila shared her last bites with him as a way to say sorry about the handprints. They all sat in a companionable silence. The sun was pleasantly warm on their faces. A bumblebee flew in lazy circles around the pot of jam, and a light breeze brought with it the salty smell of the sea. The Bedell, as usual, did not eat. Instead, he told them stories of the island, back in the day when the sea was full of seals and every night on the stony beaches there were bonfires around which dark-haired humans sang and danced until daybreak.

"And when the sun rose," he explained, "the fires

were but gray ash, and the people were gone. All that was to be seen were the seals, far out to sea, playing and diving in the blue water."

"It sounds like a wonderful place to live," Gus said. She was lying on her belly on the warm rock, resting the side of her face on her crossed arms.

"Oh, it was, it was." The Bedell's voice sounded sad.

"I wish it was like that now," Ila said dreamily. She was leaning on the Bedell, her face sticky with tea and crumbs.

"And I as well," he said. He smoothed Ila's hair away from her forehead.

"The battle between the Folk and the what's-his-name," Gus said, changing the subject. "What happened next?"

"Well, the Sea Folk were mostly gone by then, either killed in the battle or Turned to their animal forms forever. This island that used to be full of life became home to only one. The Watcher. And me."

"And our mom," said Ila.

"And Rosemaris, yes, of course."

"And now the Móraí keeps the Dobhar-chú prisoner?" Leo asked.

"Yes. Her power holds the creature fast."

"How did his wolves get free?" Leo asked. "To track us, I mean."

A shadow passed over the Bedell's face. "The Móraí is very old," he said. "And her power is weakening. She was ill this winter. So ill she almost died. Because of that, the fog slipped. Just a bit, and just once. It was not enough to allow the King of the Black Lakes to escape. But it was enough for the creature to loose some of his wolves."

"That's why the storms are getting worse, isn't it?" Leo said. "She's getting weaker." The Bedell did not answer.

"If she's so old," Gus said, "what happens when she's gone?"

The Bedell shuddered. Ila jumped up with a small scream as a furry creature spat and hissed on the rock next to her. Then the Bedell was back, pale-faced, with beads of sweat across his forehead.

"My apologies," he said.

"OK," Ila said, and seated herself back down next to the little man.

Gus was watching the Bedell closely. She opened her mouth to ask her question again, but before she could, Ila spoke.

"Are you the only Messenger?" she asked.

The little man smoothed his green waistcoat with one hand, rather like an animal smoothing its fur with a paw.

"I am," he said proudly. "The Folk have used Messengers before, of course, but usually they have been birds. The Mórai needed a Messenger who could swim as well as travel overland. Someone clever, and quick, and brave. At least, that is what she told me," he added modestly.

"Could someone take a boat here?" Leo asked.

The Bedell snorted. "Oh dear me, no," he said. "They

would pass right by this place. This is not a train station, after all! One cannot just come and go. The Watcher must stay here, and no one else may come. Except, of course, for me."

"Mr. Bedell," Leo said. "Um, I was wondering—that is, *we* were wondering—if maybe you could do that thing again? If we could be seals again?"

"And a fox," Ila said.

"And a fox," said Leo, who was still feeling kindly toward Ila after the sharing of the scone.

"Well . . . ," the Bedell said slowly.

"You could do it, right?" Gus said. "I mean, you're pretty much Folk yourself," she added coaxingly.

"Ah well, the next best thing, perhaps," the little man said, but the tips of his ears were glowing pink and he looked very pleased. He smoothed his waistcoat one more time and said, "I would have to ask the Móraí, of course."

"Please ask her," Gus said. "Oh please!"

The little man nodded slowly. "I cannot see the harm in it. I shall ask her tonight, if you like."

They packed up the picnic quickly, each of the children feeling a thrill of joy at the thought of Turning again. Then, with the Bedell close behind, they wandered back to the meadow at the top of the island, the one with the broken houses. There had been thirteen of them, the Bedell told them, set in a semicircle that faced the ocean. There were treasures to be found in the dirt—bits of broken crockery and polished green glass. Ila even found a tiny teacup half buried in the soil near one of the stone foundations.

"Look, Gus," she said. "It's so little!"

The teacup was white porcelain, with a spray of pink roses painted on one side of it. When Ila held it up, the sun shone right through its delicate edges. They continued to dig and found more pieces of china, but everything else was broken and scattered. Only the teacup had remained intact. It made Gus think of the long-ago child who had played with the tea set. *Where is she now?* she wondered.

"Let's bring it to the Mórai," Leo said, but the Bedell shook his head.

"Leave it where it belongs."

In the end, they put the teacup in a slight hollow in the rock wall and filled it with buttercups. They stepped back together to admire their work.

The cup looked pretty, overflowing with the tiny yellow flowers, but in the lonely, mournful way that a memorial might look both beautiful and sad at the same time.

At dinner, no one mentioned the stone foundations, or the little teacup. The Bedell had promised to speak to the Mórai after supper, so the children didn't dare bring up the subject of Turning, or seals, or Folk, for fear of ruining his efforts on their behalf.

Leo talked, instead, about his turtles. He was worried about their training. "People think they have long memories," he explained to the Mórai, "but they forget their tricks really fast if you don't work with them."

"I'm sure the turtles are fine," she reassured him as Gus and Ila snickered.

They went to bed early, with a kiss from the Mórai and a wink and a significant nod from the Bedell. Lying in the small bed across from Ila's, Gus realized that she felt at home on Loup Marin, in a way that she was not sure she could explain. It was just that when she woke up in the morning and smelled the fresh sea air, she wanted to leap out of bed. And at night, snuggled in under the heavy cotton coverlet, she listened to the boom of the waves against the rocky shore and felt safe and content. And the next day they would be able to swim in the breakers and explore the deep water and dive and play . . . She fell asleep in the middle of imagining just how wonderful it was going to be.

At breakfast, the Mórai said that the Bedell could take them down to the sea as soon as he returned from hunting, but by the time they had finished eating, he had not appeared. They made their beds, cleaned up from breakfast, and polished glass and brass fittings in the lighthouse, but there was still no sign of the little man.

Outside, gray rain poured down and the waves smashed monotonously against the rocks. Irritable, bored, and restless, the three children roamed around the living room, turning the pages of old books and playing an endless game of checkers that they had to start over every time Ila cheated, which was often. She was currently jumping all of Leo's pieces, her chubby hand gripping the red checker in her fist.

"Cheating," Leo said with a sigh, reaching out to reclaim his lost black checkers. "You can't jump around the board, Ila. You can only jump one space, remember? One space."

Ila growled and swept her arm across the board, scattering checkers all over the woven rug.

Leo lunged for her and got a handful of red curls, which made Ila scream and twist around to bite her brother's arm.

"Brat!" Leo shouted, letting go of Ila's hair. Ila danced out of the way and stuck her tongue out.

"Enough!" It was the Móraí, and although she was speaking quietly, it was clear that she was angry.

"Ila, come with me. You can help me cook dinner. Leo, that is not at all what I expect of you. Not at all."

Taking Ila firmly by the hand, she led her back to the kitchen.

"Little brat," Leo said grumpily to Gus. "I wish she'd at least learn to play a board game without cheating or crying or wrecking the board."

They decided to explore the books that were shelved in the tall bookcase near the sofa. It was Leo's idea. Gus was skeptical. It didn't really sound like her idea of a good time.

"Maybe we'll find some information about the Folk," Leo argued, shoving his glasses up on his nose.

Gus rolled her eyes, but she was sick of checkers and tired of watching out the window for any sign that the weather might be changing, so she reluctantly agreed to join "the hunt," as Leo insisted on calling it. After a while, she drifted over to the comfiest armchair and pretended to read a heavy clothbound book while she watched the gray sea toss and crash.

Leo didn't notice. He was too busy paging through the books, sometimes reading bits out loud, sometimes silently. Suddenly he said Gus's name.

"What?" Gus said guiltily. She picked up the book that had fallen closed on her lap and quickly read a few sentences. It seemed to be about the familial lines of mussels.

"Look at this, Gus. It's really weird."

Gus sleepily pushed herself out of her chair and walked over to where Leo was sitting on the floor. In his lap was a large book, bound in plain brown leather. Its cover was blank.

"What's so special about that?" Gus said, reaching out to touch it.

It was *warm*. Frowning, she placed her palm on the cover, just to be sure. The book was definitely warm, as though it had been lying in the sun all afternoon. Gus checked the window. Rain fell in steady sheets past the glass. Then, with a gasp, she yanked her hand away.

Leo grinned at her. "Yup. It's breathing."

"Don't be ridiculous," Gus said. "It's a book."

"So touch it again."

Gus hesitated. Of course it couldn't be breathing. But then what had she felt when she laid her hand flat on the blank cover? As if it could sense her hesitation, the book on Leo's lap seemed to sigh and *stretch*, like a cat looking to be stroked. Gus blinked. Books didn't stretch. Or move. Or breathe. But even as she watched, the plain brown book sighed and settled down more deeply into Leo's lap.

"Oh my gosh," she whispered.

Leo grinned. "Yep." He stroked the book like a tabby.

"What's inside?" Gus was almost afraid to ask. She reached out one finger, tentatively, and touched the warm brown leather. It was definitely rising and falling, for all the world like a creature asleep.

CHAPTER 15

The Book of the Folk

Leo opened the book. The inside was in complete contrast to the simple brown cover. Color seemed to leap off the page and flood the room. *The Book of the Folk* was written on the first page in a thick, glowing gold script that blazed against a vivid blue background like rays of sun lighting a morning sky. Dark green vines twined around the letters, with bright orange poppy-like flowers bursting out against the green. The vines reached down below the letters to meet a navy sea splashed here and there with frothy white breakers. The flowers moved on the vines, as though in a gentle wind, bowing and bending toward the sea. And wherever one of the blooms touched the surface of the sea, it disappeared and was replaced with the sleek, dark-eyed head of a seal.

"It's beautiful," Gus whispered, her fear forgotten. She reached out to touch the picture, but Leo was already turning the page.

The book told the story of the Folk. Leo and Gus read

about their coming, so long ago now that the time was lost to history. They read about the laws of the Folk. For the Folk, when you are twelve, you are an adult. When you are ten, you are a child. But when you are eleven, you are in the changing year, neither child nor adult. It is the year that the Folk children begin to Turn without assistance, and from then on they lead a life split between the land and the sea. But any Folk who completely leave the sea lose their connection to the others and can no longer Turn.

"Mom," Gus said, feeling a pang of sadness for their mother, for what she had had to sacrifice to make a life with their father.

The book talked about the other creatures of the sea who lived in harmony with the Folk. The dark-haired finfolk, and the singing mermaids who sometimes fell in love with humans and took them to live underwater with them forever. There were also the carnivorous water ponies, the kelpies. They were wild creatures, and danger-ous. The seals gave them a wide berth. But occasionally one of the Folk in human form would tame one of the wild ponies and ride it over the foam, only to flee from the same creature when back in its seal form.

Leo turned the pages carefully as schools of fish ap-peared and disappeared and birds shrieked and dove and flapped away carrying struggling silver bodies in their claws. They read about an island where many Folk lived, sometimes as humans, sometimes as seals.

"It's Loup Marin!" Gus whispered. She recognized

the description of the broad, flat meadow that sat at the top of the island, in which a semicircle of thirteen tidy cottages was said to face the sea. They read about rocky outcroppings covered with shining seals, sheer rock cliffs that dropped into coves, women who combed their long dark hair in the sun as children with round brown eyes ran naked in the surf, laughing. Gus and Leo laughed with them, in sheer delight. The room filled with the smells of kelp and salt water and crisp, fresh air.

It was impossible to know how much time had passed. The fire popped and hissed in the hearth, burning itself out, but neither Gus nor Leo noticed. Their heads remained bent over the book on Leo's lap as the afternoon deepened, unnoticed, around them.

An illustration showed a woman with dark hair coming out of one of the thirteen houses. She held a small baby in her arms. The woman walked across the meadow to where the lighthouse stood, except that there was no lighthouse. There was no red-roofed cottage either. Instead, there were wild, thorny bushes and a twisting path that had been worn down to dirt by countless feet passing along it. The woman worked her way down the path as it curled through the rocks to the beach below. She stood on the rocky beach, now deserted and empty of seals, and looked out at the sea. The woman looked like the Mórai, only much, much younger. The expression on her familiar face was one of fear.

The colors on the pages of the book darkened, shot through here and there with green light. Larger shapes moved more slowly now, dim on the suddenly murky paper. The long gray body of a shark flicked across the page, making Gus lean away in fear.

On the left-hand page, something shifted way down in the deep of the sea. Then a great shadow slid across the page. The shadow spread like spilled ink, and as it did, an oily, rancid stench rose off the book, so thick it seemed to blacken the air with greasy soot.

"Ugh!" Gus said, covering her nose and mouth against the stink of rot. "Close it, Leo!"

The dark shadow passed over the right-hand page and disappeared, as though traveling to the next page in the book, leaving behind it still, flat, empty water. A yellow sun shone at the top of the page. Crisp, sweet salt air blew across their faces.

The Móraí sat down at her end of the table, a mug of tea in front of her. At the other end of the table sat the Bedell. He let out a gentle burp and a white feather drifted from his mouth and landed on his empty plate. Ila giggled and the Bedell winked at her.

The memory of the dark shadow moving across the pages of the book had dulled Gus's appetite. She fiddled with her spoon and then looked over to Leo for direction. Should they say something about their discovery? Her brother had his face at the edge of his steaming bowl of soup and was snarfling up great spoonfuls. Gus sighed in irritation. The soup in front of her *did* smell good, though. She took one sip, and then another. Soon she was buttering a thick slice of brown bread to sop up the last bits in her bowl.

"Now dessert," the Móraí said when the empty bowls had been cleared away. She stood up and went into the kitchen, asking Ila to help her.

"No candles, I'm afraid," she said, coming back into the room with a white-frosted chocolate cake. Ila followed her with a small stack of plates. She had forks balanced on top of them and was concentrating very hard on keeping the stack from wobbling.

"Surprise!" Ila said. "Happy birthday!"

One by one, the forks began to slide off the plates. While Ila scrambled about on the floor, the Móraí cut generous slices of cake for everyone, even for herself and the Bedell.

"I totally forgot," Leo said. "Happy birthday, Gus."

"Happy birthday," Gus said back to him. She had forgotten as well.

Ila popped up with the forks. She gave one to the Bedell, who stared at it and then, somewhat awkwardly, stabbed at his piece of cake.

Ila giggled. "Eat it!" she commanded, and so, with a theatrical sigh, the Bedell put a forkful of cake in his mouth.

"Mmm," he said as he chewed. "Better even than seagull!"

Ila looked very pleased, and did not seem to notice that the Bedell did not take another bite of his cake.

"Oh, and we have to sing!" she said.

The Mórai looked puzzled. "Sing?"

"'Happy Birthday,'" Ila explained, and launched into the song as though she had been singing it, instead of merely listening to it, her whole life.

Gus and Leo joined in, and their voices filled the small room. The Mórai watched them with a smile on her face.

When they were finished singing, however, her smile faded. She looked down the table at the Bedell. "I think I should be alone with the children, my Messenger," she said gently. "This is only for the Folk to hear."

The Bedell sat very still. One cuff on his white shirt had a smear of chocolate across it. "Mistress?" he said softly.

"Please," she said.

The Bedell put his fork down, very carefully, next to his still-full plate and said, "Yes. Yes, of course."

He rose stiffly from his chair and left the room.

"Why did you do that?" Ila demanded. "You hurt his feelings!"

"My Messenger understands why I do what I do," the Mórai said, but none of the children were quite sure that she was right. For a moment, Gus didn't know that she even liked the Mórai. She glanced up and caught the old woman gazing steadily at her. Gus blushed and looked down hurriedly, afraid that the Mórai could read her thoughts.

"We have much to talk about," the Mórai said. "Please listen closely."

Gus and Leo both put down their forks. Ila took a quick extra bite and then put hers down too, struggling to chew the enormous mouthful of cake.

"You wanted to know why you are here," the Móraí said. "Why I sent my Messenger for you."

The children nodded.

"I brought you here for your protection," the old woman said. "Gus and Leo, as you approached your eleventh birthday, we became aware of you. I was overjoyed when my Messenger told me that Rosemaris lived and that she had three children. But as we became aware of you, so did the Dobhar-chú. I think he sent his servants to find you."

"The wolves?" Gus asked.

The Móraí nodded.

"Is that what we saw in the book?" Gus asked.

"What book?" Ila demanded.

"What did you see?" the Móraí said.

Gus wasn't sure how to describe it. "We saw a dark shadow," she said slowly, "under the water. It turned the sea black. And it stank."

"Like dead fish and hamburger grease," Leo offered.

The Móraí nodded. "Yes. That was the Dobhar-chú. What else did the book show you?"

"We read about the Folk," Leo said. "And how you learn to Turn when you're eleven." He shot a quick look at Ila, who was beginning to look like a thundercloud. "And how the Folk lived and the rules of Turning."

Ila squeezed her eyes shut and screamed.

The Móraí jumped, but Gus and Leo just rolled their eyes.

"She wants attention," Gus explained.

Two fat tears rolled down Ila's cheeks.

"No, she doesn't," the Móraí said. "She wants to be included. Come here, child." She gestured to Ila, who swiped at her cheeks with the backs of her chubby hands and slid off her chair. Gus and Leo were amazed to see her climb up on the old woman's lap.

"Now you may ask me a question," the Móraí said to Ila.

"What does the Dobhar-chú want?" Ila asked.

"He wants the sea and everything in it," the Móraí said. "I am very, very old, children. I am all that holds the Dobhar-chú fast, and I will not live much longer. When I am gone, he will be free. The rising tides and the missing fishing boats tell me that his power is growing as mine wanes. But these things are merely the shows of temper of an imprisoned monster. Once he is loose, he will bring death and destruction to anything that lives in the sea, or near it."

"More missing boats?" Gus asked.

"More than that. Remember, the Femori rule the storms, and the Dobhar-chú is stronger and crueler than his father's people. He will drown the land and make it his."

"Tsunamis," Leo said, suddenly remembering the conversation with their father. What had he said? That it would be virtually impossible for a tsunami to hit the coast of Maine? But his father hadn't known what was waiting in the sea.

"That's why Mom was trying to hide us," Leo said. "Because of the Dobhar-chú."

"I think your mother was using the song that you call the night poem," the Móraí explained. "Your mother gave up her Folk aspects when she left this island. Using a weapon like the night poem was a very dangerous thing to do. It is powerful, but it takes a bit of your strength every time you call on it. She used it too much, and she went too far. And because she has been away from here so long, the song only partially worked. As you grew older, your Folk aspects grew stronger. That is why the Bedell—and the King of the Black Lakes—was able to find you."

"But why would the Dobhar-chú care about us?" Gus asked. "I mean, we're just kids, right?"

"You are," the Móraí said, "and you are not. You are Folk, and when I die, you will be the last of the Folk."

"But what do we do now?" Gus said. "We can't just hide here forever!"

The Móraí nodded. "I am not strong enough to destroy the Dobhar-chú on my own. All I can do is keep him contained. But now that you three are here, we have a chance."

"Whoa," Leo said. "Are you talking about us fighting the Dobhar-chú? That's crazy."

"As long as the Dobhar-chú lives, your mother will continue to weaken. And if we do not destroy him, then when I am gone, he will be released from his prison."

"Mom," Gus said, and her eyes filled with tears.

"I will be with you," the Móraí said. "I have been waiting for many, many years for someone to help me to defeat the King of the Black Lakes. Now I think that the one I have been waiting for is actually three. Three Lost Children. You are here, and it is time."

Ila climbed down from the Móraí's lap and went to stand next to Gus, pressing up against her. Gus put an arm around her shoulders. Then Leo was beside her as well, standing close enough that their shoulders touched.

"OK," Leo finally said. "I guess we'll do it. Teach us how to destroy the Dobhar-chú."

CHAPTER 16

Reading at Night

"So then we just kill the what's-his-name," Gus said. She was sitting in her bed in her red nightie. Ila and Leo were perched on the end.

"But how?" Ila asked, holding Bear very tightly to her.

"We can do it," Leo said confidently.

He put out his hand. Gus put her hand on top of his.

"Come in, Ila," Gus said. Ila put Bear down and added her small hand to the pile.

"Together," Leo said.

"Together," Ila and Gus repeated.

They sat like that for a moment without moving. It felt good, somehow. None of them knew what would happen. They didn't know how or even if they would get home again. But they would do it together.

"So we have to figure out a way to fight the Dobharchú," Leo said. "It's our only option."

"The Móraí said she would teach us stuff," Gus said, but her voice sounded a bit doubtful.

"We can ask the Bedell," Ila said suddenly. "He'll know what to do. We can ask him in the morning."

Gus and Leo looked at their sister, a little startled. Ila picked up Bear and squeezed him.

So it was agreed that they would talk to the Bedell at breakfast. Everyone felt better after the plan was made, even though it wasn't much of one. Ila disappeared under her covers like a creature curling in a burrow, and Leo drifted off to his room. He thought it would take him forever to fall asleep, but instead he had barely switched off his light before he was in a deep, dreamless darkness.

When Leo woke, he did not know where he was. No blue night-light glowing cozily from the far side of the room, no bedside lamp, no sound of the oak tree's branches against his window.

He sat up, frightened, and remembered where he was. Loup Marin. Then he remembered the rest of it—the water and the swimming and the Móraí's announcement and the book . . . the book. Leo had never seen anything like *The Book of the Folk* before. For him, the chance to look again through *The Book of the Folk* was like an astrophysicist being invited on a tour of Mars. It was irresistible.

Leo swung his feet onto the cold floor. Moving as quietly as he could, he felt around for his backpack and took his small penlight out. Pulling on socks, he padded down the darkened hallway, feeling his way along the wall. He didn't dare to turn on the flashlight until he was in the living room, standing next to the velvet couch. Then, pointing the light down, he followed its beam to the bookshelf and swept it over the books. And again, and then again.

"No," he whispered. The book was gone.

Leo swung the light around and checked the floor, side tables, couch, and then the wooden trunk that served as a coffee table. *The Book of the Folk* was on the trunk. Its cover was no longer plain brown leather. Instead, the title blazed across it in gold letters that flickered like fire. Leo sank to his knees in front of the book.

Slowly, he reached out one hand. The book shivered as his hand came closer. He could feel the heat coming off it.

"May I?" he whispered. The book fell open in front of him, and feeling absurdly grateful, Leo bent his head to read.

After a moment, he clicked off the flashlight. The book was giving off its own light, and it was more than enough to read by. Its pages told the story of the great battle between the Sea Folk and the Dobhar-chú. Leo read for a long time, turning the pages quickly as the battle unfolded, scourging the seabed and staining the ocean red.

A chill wind suddenly blew out of the book, bringing with it a low, dull roar that rose off the page. It was very quiet, as though coming from a great distance, but Leo could make out different sounds within the noise—the screaming of people and the crashing of waves on rocks and the roaring of a beast and the bellowing of seals.

He read about how the Folk called the creatures of the sea to come to their aid, the ways in which they convinced the solitary squid and the wild seabirds to help them in their struggle. Silvery dolphins, great blue-finned tuna that cut through the water like living swords, black-finned killer whales, powerful blue whales, and flashing, darting otters all fought for the Folk.

The huge eels from the deepest sea went with the Dobhar-chú, as did the hammerhead and great white sharks. And there were other creatures fighting for the Dobhar-chú. The Muirbrech, a green-skinned water serpent who could hypnotize any creature with its one eye, fought for the King of the Black Lakes. Murcats, the sea cats who were the size of horses and had tusks like boars, also joined his side. There were pictures of other, unnamed creatures—a bright orange wingless dragon with an eel-shaped head, and a huge, flat creature with four eyes on its top and a long tail that ended in a set of claws that glowed silver. A black fish with a giant, sucking mouth lined with jagged teeth flashed across the page, followed by a giant blue squid with fins alternating with tentacles that wrapped around its own body so that only its blazing yellow eyes showed. And then an animal that Leo recognized. It shook the water off of its thick, reddish fur and stared up from the page with bright, malevolent eyes.

"The sea minks," Leo whispered as the animal hunched its back and hissed.

The battle might have been won and the King of

the Black Lakes defeated, Leo read, if the other magical creatures—the kelpies, the mermaids, and the finfolk—had not refused to help the Folk. But they did refuse. The battle, they told the Folk, was not theirs. An image passed over the page then, showing dark-haired men and pale women with fish tails sinking slowly beneath the surface, followed by galloping ponies who kicked up white foam with their heels before they dove. They were lost to the world, Leo read, never to be seen again.

The image shifted. The new picture showed the sea, but it was a red sea, tinged with blood from battle. The orange dragon floated across one section of the page, its body torn and bloody. He could see the flat fish with the silver claws as well. And everywhere there were seals. Their ripped coats were brown, gray, mottled, and the pure white of babyhood, all floating and jostling like so much driftwood, carried along by the currents.

The story was woven around the pictures in brilliant cursive lettering. Leo read about the imprisonment of the Dobhar-chú, and the terrible price that the Folk paid. Those who did not die in the battle disappeared. They left behind only one person, the Watcher, whose job it was to watch over the imprisoned monster and maintain the impenetrable fog that encircled the Dobhar-chú's island. The book did not mention the little girl Rosemaris, trained by the Watcher to take her place. But it did mention something else. As Leo read, he felt the hair on the back of his neck prickle with fear. There was a prophecy.

The prophecy said that whoever killed the Dobhar-chú would be cursed. That person would die within a day of the creature's death.

As Leo read, the sea mink, moving as quietly as a mote of dust, slid through the living room and out the front door. Leo lifted his head at the *snick* of the front door latching. He peered into the darkness around him, but saw nothing moving. When he looked back at the book, the words were fading on the page. Then the light coming from the book softened and went out, leaving Leo sitting in the cold, with the book quiet on the trunk. He heard rather than saw its cover close.

Leo stayed there until a dull gray light began to fill the room with early morning. The writing on the cover of the book was gone, leaving only plain, somewhat battered leather. Finally, he stood up. Without glancing at the book on the trunk, he left the living room. His head felt heavy, and something in him ached. Moving stiffly from kneeling for so long, he went back to his room and crawled into bed.

While Leo tossed and turned in the early morning, the Messenger moved low and swift through the woods. He was the Messenger, and he had come to feel that he was one of the Folk. He was the one who should be training to defeat the King of the Black Lakes, not three children who did not yet even Turn on their own. But the last few days had shown him what he truly was: an outsider, an extra, a thing with no true family. The children were allowed—no, *invited*—to hear the poem of protection, something that had always been forbidden to the Bedell. They were privy to the secrets of the Folk, while he was sent from the table like a child that was too young to hear anything of import. They probably laughed at him, the poor Bedell, sent away to slink through the darkness alone! For he *was* alone, and he felt the true weight of that solitude settle on him for the first time in his long life.

The Bedell came out at dawn by the small beach where he had landed with the children. It had been just a few days ago, but it felt like forever.

For a long time, a small man in a dapper green suit stood looking across the gray water of the Atlantic. Then with one last look back, a sea mink slipped into the water and began to swim toward his fate. It had been waiting for him, all these many years. It was time to go and meet it.

CHAPTER 17

Secrets of the Book

When Leo woke up, the sun was streaming in his window. He jumped out of bed and ran across the hall to the girls' bedroom, but they were not there. He found them in the kitchen, eating breakfast. The Bedell was not at the table. Neither was the Móraí.

Leo sat down in front of a bowl of steaming oatmeal topped with chopped apples and a puddle of honey. He took a large bite and then said, "We need to talk."

"Do you mind swallowing first?" Gus said crankily.

Leo swallowed and was about to tell Gus and Ila about what he had seen in the book the night before, but telling them what he had read would mean telling them he had snuck out of bed without them. His indecision was resolved for him when the Móraí came into the room. He was definitely not yet ready to confess to the Móraí.

Gus spoke first. "We've decided," she said as the Móraí settled into her chair. "We'd like you to train us. We want to fight the Dobhar-chú."

The Mórai nodded. "Very well. We will begin to-night, when the moon is full." She looked at the empty chair where the Bedell usually sat. "Has the Messenger been here?" she asked.

"No," Gus said. "And he's supposed to take us back to the sea."

The Mórai smiled. "I'm sure he'll turn up. Would you girls mind clearing the table while Leo and I go to the lighthouse? There was a problem last night with one of the lenses."

"Sure," Gus said. "Then can we look for the Bedell?"

"Yes, you may," the old woman said. "Leo?"

Leo hastily shoved a last spoonful of oatmeal into his mouth and followed the Mórai out of the kitchen.

They fixed the lens, which had come loose from its mounting, and then polished all the brass fittings with soft cloths until they gleamed. Leo tried to tell the Mórai what he had read and seen in *The Book of the Folk*. But every time he opened his mouth to say something, his courage failed him. When he finally did say something, he surprised himself by asking, "What was my mom like? I mean, as a little girl?"

The Mórai paused at the window, where she was clean-ing the glass. "Well, she looked exactly like Gus, but her temper was more like Ila's. She wanted to do everything, right from the start. She was so impatient to turn eleven!"

"I think Ila can almost Turn by herself," Leo said. "I mean, she fought with the Bedell when he tried to Turn her back, and she almost won."

The Mórai smiled. "She's very strong," she said. "But your mother, she was also like you."

"How was she like me?" Leo said eagerly.

"Well, she was always sketching and drawing. Everything she saw, she had to put down in her notebook."

"Oh," Leo said, feeling disappointed. "But I can't draw."

"No, I didn't mean that. I meant she was the way that you are about your books. Always looking, always wanting to know things, always trying to learn more and understand more. She was very like you in that respect."

"She isn't really your daughter, is she?" Leo said. "I mean, if you were around at the time of the great battle and all."

The Mórai looked at him sharply. "How did you know that?" she asked.

Leo tried to drive the image of the book out of his head. "I don't know," he said vaguely. "You must have told us, I guess."

"Hmm," the Mórai said, looking unconvinced. "No," she added after a moment, "I am not your grandmother. I am something like your great-great-great-great-grandmother, I suppose."

"Do you miss her?" Leo asked.

The Mórai nodded. "I do," she said.

They did not talk again after that. Eventually, the Mórai left Leo to his work. He didn't even notice the time passing until the setting sun lit the small room with vivid pink light.

Dinner was quiet. Leo was preoccupied with thoughts of what the Móraí was going to teach them. Gus and Ila were sunburned and tired from searching for the Bedell all day. They had not found him. When they were done eating, all three children looked expectantly at the Móraí. Outside, the moon had risen, fat and full. It was time.

"Gus," the Móraí said, "please go and get the book that you and Leo were looking at yesterday."

Leo felt his face grow hot. He pretended to be looking for his napkin under the table.

"The book that tells about the Folk?" Gus said.

"Yes. Bring it to me. Don't open it."

It took Gus a minute or two to find the book. Its plain brown cover looked the same as that of the book next to it, but when she passed her hands over the spines of the books, she could feel the heat coming off one of them. When she pulled it from the shelf, she could see the cover just barely pulsing. It was definitely the right one. She held the book lightly on her fingertips, away from her body, remembering the monsters and the sleek, steel-gray creature patrolling its pages.

"Thank you," the Móraí said as Gus laid the heavy book gently in her lap.

Leo stared down at his plate.

"Now tell me, children," the Móraí said. "What is it that humans have that the beasts do not?"

"Candy," Ila said.

"Language?" Gus guessed.

"Goodness no, child. Humans have no claim to that. Every creature speaks to its kind."

Gus blushed, feeling foolish.

Then Leo spoke, very quietly, without looking up. "Writing," he said. "And reading. Most people, that is."

"I can almost read," Ila said defensively.

The Mórai nodded. "Leo is right. When an animal is born, it is given memories from generations back, but they are faint and hazy. They feel like distant voices—like what you might call *instinct*. But humans, because they can read and write, can capture memories. They can send their thoughts across space and through time, even to generations not yet born. It's a kind of immortality. It's powerful, powerful magic."

Gus and Leo had learned in school of the great library of Alexandria, in Egypt, burned to the ground thousands of years ago. At the time Gus had wondered idly about the books and stories lost to the flames. But now she wondered what else had perished—what memories, what warnings, what spells and magics had gone up in the orange heat of the marauding fires. It seemed, suddenly, like an incalculable loss. The Mórai interrupted her thoughts.

"And it is more than that. This book not only tells the tales of battles won or lost, it tells of your family, your blood that stretches back thousands of years and circles the globe. There is power in the stories. It's the same power that connects you three—the love you share."

"Well, maybe," Leo said, forgetting his guilt over the

book for a moment. "You have no idea how annoying sisters can be."

"Who chews like a pig?" Gus asked.

"Yeah," Ila said. "A snorty, porky pig."

She and Gus sniggered.

"See what I mean?" Leo said pointedly.

Gus's face became serious. "What about the other creatures?" she asked the Mórai. "The water ponies, and—"

Ila interrupted her. "Water ponies!" she said excitedly. "Could I ride them?"

"No way," Leo told her. "Not these ponies. They'd rip you apart and eat you."

Ila looked skeptical. "They'd eat me?"

"They're actually called *kelpies*," Leo said. "And everything you read says that kelpies are carnivorous."

Ila narrowed her eyes.

Gus spoke quickly before Leo said anything more about reading. "But where are they?"

The Mórai looked sad. "They are long gone, I'm afraid. The kelpies, the mermaids, the finfolk. All gone now."

"The book said they wouldn't help in the battle," Leo said.

"I don't remember that part," Gus said. "Where did it say that, Leo?"

"Um, somewhere in there," Leo said, blushing. "I was reading pretty fast. I probably read a little more than you did."

The Mórai gave Leo a sharp look but said nothing.

"What exactly *is* that book?" Gus asked.

"It's the story of the Folk," the Mórai said. She opened the book, and Ila hopped down and went to the end of the table to climb up on the old woman's lap.

"Is that gold?" she asked.

Gus and Leo both crowded around Ila and the Mórai to look at the book. Instead of monsters or corpses or a blood-red sea, this page simply showed a tree. It was an oak tree with an emerald-green trunk and long, branching arms covered in leaves of gold that had been shaped and affixed to the paper. The trees branches snaked over both of the open pages, filling every bit of white space with gleaming gold. Ila reached out one hand.

"Ila, don't!" Gus said, but it was too late. Ila's fingers brushed one of the leaves.

"It feels real," she said in amazement.

As she spoke, the leaf curled itself closed and then re-opened, unfurling as a flower, with each gold petal opening independently. The tree shivered on the page with a sound like a sigh, and every leaf on every branch closed and unfurled until the tree was hung with shimmering gold flowers.

"Oh!" Ila said, but the page was not done changing. At the center of each flower was an image. Gus saw an ocean in one, flat and blue. In another was a rising sun. In other flowers, fish leapt out of sparkling seas, gulls called, and dark birds tucked their wings and dove. But most of the flowers held seals. There were seals in the bright white of infancy, mottled seals with round brown eyes, strongly built gray seals, seals sleek and dark with water, and seals lying on sunbaked rocks. The tree hummed with their voices as they called and barked and dove in the blue water. Then some of the seals, the ones who were resting on rocky outcroppings or floating with their heads just above the surface of the sea, began to sing. They sang wordless, meandering tunes that worked their way around one another like smoke from fires, winding and twisting and joining together in the air of the cottage.

Gus didn't even know she was crying until she felt the tears running in tickly streams on either side of her nose. She went to swipe at the wetness and found she was holding Leo's hands tightly in her own. Leo's own eyes were shining with tears. Ila was transfixed, her face glowing in the light from the shifting, singing, shimmering pages.

As the three children watched, the tree changed one more time. The singing, one tune now, high and sweet and wordless, grew louder and louder and then began to fall away. As the music faded, something began to form at the very top of the tree. It began as a bright green bud that burst into a gold leaf, this one much larger than the other leaves had been. All around it, the seals, fish, and birds had gone still and silent, watching from inside the frames of their own gold flowers, waiting.

Ila reached out to the strange leaf, and this time no one tried to stop her. She stroked it gently, just once. It folded on itself instantly, as the other leaves had done, and then it burst open as a great, glowing flower surrounded by six gold petals. At the center of the flower stood three children. The children were standing on a rock that rose out of a flat green sea. Behind them, a red sun was just at the horizon. Two of the children, a girl and a boy, had dark, shining hair that was colored in ink so black it was almost blue. The smallest child had fiery red hair.

CHAPTER 18

Training

"Are those children us?" Gus asked quietly.

"Yes," the Móraí said.

As they watched the page, the tree faded away, taking the creatures with it, leaving only the gold flower in which the children stood. Then words began to form under the flower, written by an invisible hand, the ink rising up fresh and clear on the page. The handwriting was some sort of ornate cursive. Each letter twisted and curled into the next like a growing vine. This time it was Leo who reached out to the book, using one finger to trace the coiling, winding letters.

"On this night," he read slowly. "This—I think it says *darkest*—this darkest hour."

"On this night, / This darkest hour!" Gus said excitedly.

"It's the night poem," Ila said.

She was right.

"Ah," the Móraí said. She read the poem out loud,

the familiar words making the children all feel, for just a moment, that their mother was near.

> On this night,
> This darkest hour
> This hearth,
> This house,
> This hold.
> On the fire
> On the bower
> On the young
> And old.
>
> From the forest
> From the fen
> From the flame
> And sea,
> Salt and iron
> Rock and den
> To fight
> To shield,
> The three.

"The three," Leo said. "What does that mean?"

"Sky, sea, and wood," the Móraí said. "At least, that was what I was taught. Now that I have met you three children, though, I am not so sure."

"Look!" Gus said. The white space on the page under the poem was filling up with the gold cursive writing.

The words looked like they belonged with the poem, but they were in a language that she had never seen before.

"What does it say?" she asked.

"I will translate it for you," the Móraí said. Speaking very softly, she read the final stanza of the night poem:

> This eve
> This night
> This endless night
> Three is many
> Weak is might
> Call the creatures
> To the light
> Oh, Lost Children, come.

"Our mother never said that part," Leo said.

"She didn't know that part," the Móraí said. "And I have never seen it either. The book is only now showing it."

"'Lost Children'?" Gus asked. "What does that mean?"

The Móraí traced her fingers over the poem. "From the flame / And sea," she read. "Salt and iron / Rock and den."

"Salt and sea and rock," Leo said. "Seals. But what about flame and iron and den?"

"Foxes," Gus said quietly.

"Foxes," Ila repeated.

"It's us," Leo said. "It's about us."

He leaned eagerly over the book again. But as he scanned it, the orange ball of the rising sun behind the children began to move. It grew larger and brighter until its light eclipsed the sea, and then the rock on which the children stood, and finally the gold flower that held the children's images. With a sound like a log popping in a blaze, the page burst into flame. Gus and Ila and Leo scrambled backward, but the Móraí sat without moving, the burning book on her lap. The flames did not touch her. They burned without heat or smoke, quickly, and then just as quickly were gone. The book was also gone. On the Móraí's lap sat a pile of silvery ash.

"Oh no!" Gus said. "The book."

The Móraí stood up, holding the hem of her pullover in front of her to form a basket for the ashes. Moving quickly, she went into the living room, the three children behind her watching as she bent over the dying fire in the hearth and dumped the ashes in. There was a flare of green light, and the slumbering embers burst back into flame, burning bright and hot—a normal fire.

The Móraí said gently, "Look on the bookshelf, children. Gus will show you where."

Hesitantly, Gus went to the place where she had found the book. Instead of an empty space, there was the familiar brown spine. Gus put her hand up and could feel the faint heat pulsing off of it.

"Best not to touch it," the Móraí said. "It will be some time before anyone will be able to open the book again."

"But how will we know what to do?" Leo's voice rose

in frustration. Ever since he was two years old, Leo had turned to books for the truth. First the truths that lay in the fairy tales: that heroes could be anyone, that right conquered wrong, that wishes might come true. Then, later, the truths of science, the way a butterfly's wing functions, or why water always runs downhill. For as long as he could remember, books had always, *always* supplied the answers that he sought.

"The book has shown you what you need," the Móraí explained. "You just have to recognize it. I will help you, as best I can."

"Can we train now?" Ila asked. "You said tonight."

The lamplight shone on the Móraí's face, lighting the network of tiny wrinkles that fanned out from her eyes and around her mouth. Her cheekbones pressed against her skin, making her look very old, and very frail. She pushed herself away from the fireplace mantel, wincing at some hidden pain.

"Come, Leo," she said. "Help me. We will go to the beach."

They followed the twisting path under the light of the full moon. Leo held the Móraí's arm as they made their way down, but still the old woman stumbled several times. Gus was feeling more and more strongly that they had to find the Bedell. The Móraí seemed to be weakening before their eyes.

They stopped on the rocks, close to the water. The moonlight threw the beach into black-and-white relief and illuminated the tide pools where the three of them had splashed around only three days before. It felt like much longer.

The Móraí stepped onto a long, low rock. Waves lashed its surface, soaking her almost to her knees, but she did not seem to notice. "Ila, take my hand," she instructed. Her voice sounded firmer now. "Gus, Leo, stand in front of me."

The children did as they were told. Gus wished she could take Leo's hand, but she didn't dare. They stood side by side on the wet rock. Cold water splashed across the backs of their legs.

"You have the history of the Folk inside you," the Móraí said. Her voice was strong now, and steady. She stood straight and tall, gripping Ila's small hand in her own. The moonlight made her silvery-white hair glow.

"Take hands," she said.

With a sense of relief, Gus gripped Leo's hand in her own. He squeezed once, hard, and she squeezed back. The wind was howling now, tearing at their clothes and whipping their hair across their faces. The Móraí had to shout over its rising sound.

"Listen closely. It will go hard the first time, but it will get easier. Empty your minds, and look at me."

What happened next was not something that Gus or Leo could ever describe, even to one another. As they looked into the dark eyes of the Móraí, she began to speak. It was a list of some sort, a list of *things*—trees, plants, bats who hugged the dusk with their leathered wings, birds who scoured mountaintops for carrion, and great dark fish who moved slowly through the loneliest parts of the sea. She spoke of the hot air of the desert as it billowed over the shifting sands, and then the cool of the icy mud at the bottom of an algae-choked pond in winter. She led them through snow, and blinding storms, onto great floating chunks of ice, and then into the torrid heat of a soaking wet jungle, all green and pungent and close.

It was not like being Turned by the Bedell. That had been a whirling kaleidoscope of confusion, a sense of being changed by something out of their control. This came from within their bodies, if they could even use that word. For it was as if their bodies had become the world. They were waves and wind and seagulls calling and slick rock etched by water and warmed by sun. They were not human, or animal, but were *world*, from their pulsing cells to the arching sky over their heads.

They were freezing, and then dying of thirst, and then gasping for breath on the tip of a mountain, and then plunging through light-specked green water. The Móraí's words passed through them, scouring them clean with sand and wind and sleet and merciless sunlight and endless darkness.

Gus and Leo cried out, a singular cry that was wrenched from deep within them, far deeper than their human minds could ever travel, as they felt the earth give way under their feet and the sky come to meet them and, at last, they Turned.

* * *

As seals, they dove for the water without thinking, slipping off the wet rock and into the welcoming black water with a sense of relief so profound it blurred into joy. Gus turned a dizzying somersault, and then another, awash in delight. She smelled salt, and mussels, and silvery fish, and the tang of seaweed. She heard waves and sighs and patters and her own heartbeat, laid over the lighter, quicker heartbeats of other creatures.

She straightened out and then dove deep, deep, deep, rocketing into the quiet of the depths, far below the wind-whipped surface. She sensed, rather than saw, that Leo was near her. Then she saw his sleek form streaking for the surface. She followed him, bursting out into the chill night air with a great whoosh, filling her lungs in the next breath. She heard someone calling her name and dimly registered two shapes on the rock, but it meant nothing to her bliss-clouded brain.

She dove again, dodging past Leo as she did, then twirled and gave quick chase to a passing school of fish. She was streaking forward, testing her speed, when a sound reached her from the surface. The sound was like a tickle at the edges of her mind, something once known, something forgotten.

Curious, Gus surfaced. She was quite close to the rocks, and she could see, even with her blurry out-of-water vision, that two people stood on the rocks. One was the Mórai, and the other was Ila, who was holding out her arms and shouting Gus's name. The sound of her sister's voice exploded like a fire inside of Gus. With a feeling like being flipped inside out, Gus Turned and found herself in the midnight Atlantic.

The waves that had carried Gus and Leo out now fought to keep Gus from returning to shore. She was knocked back again and again as she tried to swim in. Each time the waves thrust her back, she swallowed a mouthful of the cold water. Gasping and spitting, she treaded water just beyond the breaking waves, trying to gather her strength even as an icy chill spread through her, numbing her. Then a sleek, dark shape swam up next to her. Leo was still a seal. Gus forced her leaden arms around Leo's neck and closed her eyes as the seal swam them both in, diving through the waves and dumping Gus onto the wet rock where the Mórai and Ila stood. Then Leo Turned as well and scrambled up beside Gus.

Ila leapt on Gus, who managed to sit up. Wrapping her arms around her little sister, Gus held her close, murmuring, "It's OK, Ila, it's OK."

"Don't leave me!" Ila cried furiously. "It's not fair to leave me behind!"

Her hot, angry tears scalded Gus's icy skin while Gus promised, over and over, that they would never leave Ila again.

After a few minutes, the Mórai urged them up and on their feet, and led them back to the waiting house.

Inside, the three children shivered themselves into their pajamas and then went to the living room, where the Móraí waited with hot cocoa. They drank the steaming chocolate in silence. Ila would not look at Gus or Leo. She sat on the floor with her back to them and stared into the fire that blazed on the hearth.

"It will get easier," the Móraí said. "There is always a danger of being too attached to one form or another. Remember I told you that the Folk who left for the land lost their ability to Turn?"

Gus and Leo nodded. Ila did not move.

"It is also a danger in the other direction. If you choose the sea above all else, then you lose the land. That is the choice many made after the great battle."

Gus thought of the wild joy that had overtaken her under the water. She might well have turned her back on the rock where the Móraí and Ila waited. She might well have dived deep and kept on going. She gave a slight shiver at the thought.

The Móraí rose to her feet. "Gus, Leo, why don't you two go to bed. We can practice more tomorrow. Ila, stay with me for a moment, child."

Gus and Leo obediently stood. They were too tired to ask any questions, much less to protest going to bed. As they left the room, Gus turned back to see the Móraí kneeling beside Ila. Her head was so close to Ila's that the silver strands of her hair were interwoven with Ila's red curls. She was speaking very softly, too softly for Gus to hear.

Ila nodded once and then began to cry again, but this time very quietly.

Gus and Leo pulled the mattress off of Leo's bed and put it between the twin beds in the girls' room. When Ila came to bed, Gus helped her into her nightie.

"You'll be able to Turn too, Ila," she said as she fastened the buttons on the back of the nightgown. "The Mórai will help you. Now take Bear and hop into bed."

Ila grabbed Bear and, holding him tightly, climbed into her bed. Leo, lying on his mattress on the floor, told her a silly story about a cat with wings until she fell asleep with one of Bear's paws in her mouth. She looked very young, and Gus was seized again by guilt that they had almost left her forever. Because no matter what she had told Ila, she and Leo had almost gone for good.

"Do you think she's OK?" she whispered to Leo.

He nodded. "She'll be fine."

Gus wasn't convinced, but she was too tired to think more about it. She closed her eyes and dropped abruptly off into uneasy, restless dreams. Leo lay awake for a few more minutes, thinking. Then he sighed and rolled over and fell asleep as well.

But while the children slept, the Messenger returned.

CHAPTER 19

Ila's Secret

Ila had been dreaming about a puppy. It was a small white puppy with caramel-colored spots. It didn't have a name, not yet. She would be the one to choose its name, because it was hers. Not Gus's, or Leo's, but hers. And it didn't care how well she talked, or if she could read, or if she turned on lights at night like normal people always seemed to remember to do. The little puppy snuggled closer and nuzzled Ila with its damp nose. She laughed and tried to push it away, but it nuzzled her again, becoming more insistent, pushing at her face until she dropped out of the dream and opened her eyes to find herself staring into the round brown eyes of the sea mink.

Ila drew in a quick breath, but the creature shook his head, warning her to silence. His eyes gleamed in the light from the rising moon. The sea mink pushed his cold nose against her one more time and then turned and slipped through shadows to the window that was set between the two beds.

Ila looked over at Gus, and then down at Leo asleep on the mattress on the floor. They were both just lumps under their covers. The sea mink leapt lightly onto the nightstand and touched the glass of the window with his nose, and then looked at her. Moving slowly, feeling as though she might still be in a dream, Ila reached forward and unhooked the window, allowing it to swing outward into the night.

The sea mink laid his bristly muzzle against her cheek and breathed the words "Follow me. Quiet."

Then, without glancing back at her, he stretched to the open window and sprang up and out into the night. Ila looked over at Gus again, uncertain. Shouldn't she wake her? She'd be mad if Ila had an adventure without her. The thought made Ila smile. Gus *would* be mad. So would Leo. She would have a night adventure with the Bedell, maybe even turn into a fox again, and they would miss the whole thing. Then at breakfast she could just say casually, "Oh, last night when I was running through the woods with the Bedell . . . ," and their eyeballs would pop out of their heads!

Or maybe she wouldn't. Even though she had started speaking, Ila was still more comfortable with silence. Words felt prickly and difficult in her throat, like things that had to be shoved out. Talking, she was discovering, was *tiring*.

She couldn't say why she had not spoken most of her life, or why she was speaking now. Both Gus and Leo had asked her about it, at separate times, but all she could tell them was that for a while she wanted to be quiet, and now she wanted to speak. It was as simple as that, really. Her answer hadn't satisfied either of them. And she could tell they still thought she was a bit of a weirdo, even if she could talk.

And then there was what had happened on the beach. Gus said they would never leave her, but Ila wasn't so sure. She had watched the seals leap joyfully into the waiting sea. The thought brought a jolt of pain with it, so she turned to something else. They had looked at the book the first time without her! She forgot that she had been sent out of the room for biting and instead just felt the heat of being left out *again*. That heat was enough to propel her up onto the nightstand and the windowsill.

But as she leaned out the open window, Ila suddenly remembered the Móraí. She might be mad too. She might punish her, even. But the Móraí had said she was special. Not *weird*, but *special*. And special meant you got to do special things, like sneak out in the night. So Ila boosted herself over the windowsill, landing on her hands and knees in the cool, damp grass.

She scrambled to her feet, drying her palms on her nightie. The moon was up and the air smelled like salt and wet grass. The Bedell was in his human form.

"Where have you been?" Ila asked. "We looked all over for you!"

Instead of answering her, the Bedell put a finger to his lips. "Follow me to the beach," he whispered.

"But wait," Ila whispered back. "I want to be a fox."

"Not now," he answered. "Just follow me."

Ila felt her face getting hot. Her adventure was supposed to be as a fox, not as a kid in a stupid nightgown.

"No," she said. "I won't."

The Bedell stepped closer and leaned down to Ila.

"Ila," he said very quietly but with an edge of urgency. "We must catch the tide."

"I only like the fox," Ila said. "And I want to be one, now."

"Listen to me, you silly thing," the Bedell hissed.

Ila drew back, frightened.

The Bedell took a deep breath. "My apologies," he said, with a slight bow. "But time is of the essence, Ila."

"I don't know what that means," Ila said, glancing back toward the open window. Maybe she could scramble up without Gus and Leo hearing her come in. She could just crawl back into bed and no one would know that she had even been gone.

The Bedell began speaking very quickly and so quietly that Ila had to lean toward him to hear his words. "It means we have to hurry if you want to help."

Ila said nothing. Her plan to roam the woods as a fox and return triumphant for breakfast was rapidly fading.

"Me?" she finally said. "I'm the smallest. I can't even Turn yet."

"But you are the strongest," the Bedell said. "You have the blood of three forms in you, Ila. That makes you very strong indeed. The question is, are you brave enough to do this? I can help you, but you must be brave. You are the only one who can save your mother, Ila."

"I can save my mom?" Ila said. "How? Tell me!"

She took a step toward the Bedell, her hands fisted.

He smiled but took a step backward. "Now, now," he said soothingly. "We just have to go to the island where the Dobhar-chú is held prisoner and defeat him. You are strong enough to do that, believe me, Ila."

"And I get to be a fox?"

"Soon," the Bedell promised. "Very soon."

"And you'll tell Gus and Leo that I did it and you only helped?"

The man sighed.

"OK," Ila said. "Let's go."

She took the Bedell's hand, which seemed to startle him.

"Ah, yes," he said. "Let us go."

The skidbladnin was waiting for them, bobbing gently on the night sea. They walked together to the end of a long, slick rock and then the Bedell hopped lightly aboard and helped Ila step onto the boat.

"Now sit," he said, and before he had finished speaking the little boat leapt forward eagerly and sped into the darkness. Ila held the Bedell's hand as she watched the water pass under them. She *could* see in the dark, better than Leo or Gus, but out here there was nothing to see.

Just water below and a faint sprinkling of stars above. After a few minutes, she curled up on the deck, still holding the Messenger's hand, and fell asleep.

The man watched her. Her small hand was limp and warm in his, but he didn't let it go. He held it tightly as they traveled, as if Ila's warmth could draw out the despair and shame and fear that poisoned his blood. The boat moved swiftly forward, and the cold wind tore the tears from his eyes before they could touch his face.

The boat bumped against something and woke Ila.

She stretched and looked around her. They were tucked into a narrow, wedge-shaped cave that the ocean had cut into a rough, reddish granite cliff. Waves crashed at the mouth of the cave, splashing the little boat. All around them was more of the red rock—great chunks of it scattered at the edge of land as though a giant child had been playing and then abandoned his blocks. When Ila peered upward, she could just see dark pine trees perched on top of the cliffs. They seemed very far away.

By standing on the edge of the boat (Ila on her tiptoes), they could scramble onto a ledge that jutted out from the side of the cave. It was only big enough for one of them to stand on, so the Bedell went first. Once he was on the ledge, he showed Ila how to climb up and out of the cave by using chunky hand- and footholds in the steep wall. Ila followed the man's instructions, and after a moment of clambering in the semidarkness, she was able to pull herself to the top of a wide, rough rock about ten feet above the crashing surf.

"Oh, you forgot the boat!" Ila said. She waited for the Bedell to scramble back down for the skidbladnin, but he just shook his head.

"It will be fine there," he said. "We have no more need of it." Then, before Ila could ask any more questions, he held out his hand to her.

"Come. There is a path from here. I know how to go."

They followed a twisty, nearly invisible path that led them up the rocky side of the island. There was a lot of jumping and climbing and scrambling, and Ila was relieved when they reached the dark pine forest. She was tired from the climb and beginning to wonder how they were ever going to find the Dobhar-chú in this forbidding place, and also how long it would be until she got some breakfast.

But in the end, they didn't have to find the King of the Black Lakes. He found them. Or rather, his wolves found them. Tall and long-legged, as gray and lean as smoke, they slipped out of the underbrush without a sound and stood in front of them.

"His wolves," the Bedell said. Ila clutched his hand, but he did not sound frightened. He sounded tired.

The wolves suddenly bent down as one, so that their chins rested on the ground and their haunches were up in the air behind them. They looked like cats stretching in the morning, except for their thick fur and their tails, which stuck up straight behind them like gray brushes. Then they rose to their feet in one silent wave, and melted backward into the thick pine trees.

The wolves had been standing in front of a small pool of water. When Ila could see what was in the pool, she took an involuntary step back, and then another.

"Ah, so," the Dobhar-chú said softly.

Ila opened her own mouth to speak, but nothing came out. She felt a wave of nausea wash over her, followed by a chill that ran down her spine and brought up goose bumps on her arms.

The body of the creature in the pool was hidden under the water. Only his head, set on a sea serpent's long, curving neck, showed. The Dobhar-chú had pointed black ears, and black lips that curled back on a dog's muzzle. But the head, bony and cadaverous, was as large as Ila's torso. There was no fur on it. Instead, black, oily skin was stretched like wet leather over the angles of the skull. Barnacles were growing in a pebbly patch on one side of his face. They had spread down from his eye onto his long muzzle, pulling his black lip on that side away from his teeth in a permanent sneer. Wet black gills fluttered along the sides of the muzzle and down the long neck. It was impossible to tell if the creature was floating or resting on the bottom of the pool. Its eyes, pure black all the way to the edges, stared unblinking at Ila and the Bedell.

When the Dobhar-chú spoke, Ila remembered what

Leo had told her once about sharks, that instead of one row of deadly teeth, they had many rows, so hundreds of teeth could fit in their mouths. He also said sharks sometimes swam up water pipes into bathtubs, so she had written the entire thing off as a lie. But now that she could see the Dobhar-chú's teeth, she understood exactly what a shark's mouth must look like. The Dobhar-chú's mouth was *full* of teeth, crammed in not only next to one another but behind as well. She forced herself to look away as the creature spoke again.

"Messenger!" the Dobhar-chú said.

The Bedell dropped Ila's hand and stepped forward.

"Bedell?" Ila said shakily.

The little man did not answer her but stood before the pool with his head bent.

"I think you should kneel before your master, Messenger," the Dobhar-chú said softly.

The Bedell dropped to one knee and bowed his head. "Master," he said, so quietly that Ila was not sure what she had heard.

"Bedell," Ila said, frightened now. "Bedell, get up!"

The man did not move, or even look in her direction.

"One more time and a little bit louder," the Dobhar-chú said.

"Master," the Bedell said, and this time his voice, though it broke on the word, rang out through the forest.

"You see," the Dobhar-chú said merrily, looking over the kneeling man's shoulder to where Ila stood. His teeth jostled for space in his mouth. "Everyone's loyalty can be bought. It's a good lesson to learn young. Consider yourself tutored."

Ila balled her hands into fists. "What are you doing?" she said to the bowed back of the Bedell. "Get up, Bedell—we have a plan. I need you!"

"Come here, child," the creature in the pool said. "Come stand beside my Messenger."

Ila stepped forward. The Bedell had betrayed them, and she had followed him, straight to the Dobhar-chú. And now Gus and Leo and the Móraí wouldn't be able to help her. She was alone.

"Good," the Dobhar-chú purred. "Now. Let me introduce myself. I am, as you probably have deduced, the Dobhar-chú."

"I know who you are," Ila said. "And I know you're stuck here on this stupid island forever. And I'm not afraid of you." The last bit was a lie. Ila had never been so afraid in her life.

The Dobhar-chú continued as if Ila had not spoken. "I was born many, many, many years ago. My mother, alas, wished only to escape me. She didn't get very far, though. No, not far at all . . ." His voiced trailed off and something like flame flickered in his eyes.

"The humans locked their doors and hid their children at the very mention of me. I took to the northern lakes, and I became the king of those waters. To be king is good, yes?"

He paused and turned his black eyes upon the Messenger, who nodded. It was just a tiny little nod, but the creature seemed satisfied.

"I was feared by all who lived. I was a story whispered around a fire. They did not dare speak my name out loud. I was alone, but I was feared. Until the Folk drove me here and imprisoned me on this rocky place. Now I am alone, and I am forgotten. No one wants to be alone, am I right, my Messenger?"

The Messenger nodded again.

"I have been looking for you, my little one, you and your brother and your sister. I had almost given up hope of getting my claws—so to speak—into you. But then your dear friend here showed up on my island! I wanted to kill him right away, but it's so rare we get company here, I decided to let him speak. And we had such a lovely chat! It seems the Bedell has been feeling a bit left out. A bit alone, shall we say, in the world. And I know all about that, don't I? So we made a bargain, your furry friend and I. You see, I had no way of getting to you three. I am, as you so charmingly pointed out, stuck here."

"How could you?" Ila said to the kneeling man beside her.

The Bedell did not answer her.

"Bedell?" she said, and her voice broke a bit on his name.

The Messenger's body shuddered.

"Oh, don't be such a fusspot, Bedell," the Dobhar-chú said teasingly. "Tell the girl what you will get from our bargain. Go on, tell her."

The Bedell said nothing.

"Messenger?" the Dobhar-chú said with a bit of an edge to his silky voice.

"I bring you the child," the Bedell said dully. "In exchange, you will bring back my family."

"Yes!" the Dobhar-chú said. Then, turning to Ila, he added, "And now that you are here, well, let's just say I think it will not be long before your sister and brother come looking for you."

"You better hope they don't," Ila said. She was pleased to hear how steady her voice sounded.

The Dobhar-chú laughed. Two teeth, each one the size of Ila's hand, fell from his open mouth and into the pool, sinking slowly beneath the surface. Two new teeth pushed forward from the row behind and filled the dark gaps in the monster's mouth.

"Child, you are fun!" he said.

He paused to spit a third tooth into the pool. "I'd almost like to keep you. But, alas, bigger plans, bigger plans! Once I am rid of you and your sister and brother, nothing will hold me on this scrubby little island."

The Dobhar-chú began to cough, a sharp, barking hack, opening his mouth and displaying giant snaggly teeth, and behind them, more teeth marching back in rows into the darkness of his throat. Then, as Ila stared in horror, a second set of jaws pushed its way forward, snapping viciously within the open mouth of the creature. The Dobhar-chú bent his long neck to the pool's surface, and as he did, the second set of jaws stretched forward and plucked a twisting, terrified striped bass from the water. The fish was huge, nearly as long as the mink, but the Dobhar-chú held the thrashing creature easily. The second set of jaws retreated, pulling the meal with it down the creature's gullet. The thrashing lump that was the fish moved down the long neck of the Dobhar-chú, who gagged and gulped like a giant cat with a hairball, swallowed hard, and cleared his throat.

"Pardon me," he said politely. "Now," the Dobhar-chú said, turning his black eyes on Ila once again. "Look up at me for just a minute, little red hair."

Ila looked down instead. She could feel her scalp prickling with the force of the creature's gaze. She stared stubbornly at the dark water in front of her and thought of Gus, of Leo, of her parents.

"Mom, Dad, Leo, Gus," she said, and then said it again, her voice thin and wobbling. "Mom, Dad, Leo, Gus."

She pictured the twins, their dark eyes, Leo's crazy cowlicks that forced his hair into spikes all over his head, the freckles sprinkled on Gus's nose. She pictured her father's way of smiling without moving his mouth. But when she tried to picture her mother, all there was in her mind's eye was a hospital bed, still and white. The white sheets were pulled tight across the empty bed, smooth and flat and final.

With a gasp, Ila opened her eyes and found herself looking into the dark eyes of the Dobhar-chú. It was like gazing into the vast night sky. Ila was smaller than a distant star, one in a multitude, all living in that dark liquid.

Then she shook her head hard, breaking the creature's gaze.

"No," she said hotly.

"Soon," he answered. "See to it, Messenger."

Without another word, he slipped down into the pool. The water closed over his head without a ripple.

Ila sprang at the Bedell. Caught unaware, he was tumbled backward by the force of her attack. She landed on him, as quick as a cat, and pounded him with her small fists, screaming with rage. The little man lay quite still and allowed her to punch him.

"You lied!" she cried in a passion of fury and grief. "I hate you, I hate you, I hate you!"

Ila flailed at the man until her arms would lift no more. And then, very gently, the Bedell sat up and took her in his arms, where she sobbed angrily and kicked at him. When even her tears were exhausted, he pulled her carefully to her feet by her wrists so that they stood facing one another next to the pool.

"I'm so sorry, Ila," he said. "Please forgive me."

And then the Messenger swung Ila into the air and dropped her into the pool where the Dobhar-chú had disappeared. She screamed once before the water closed over her head and pulled her down, to where the Dobhar-chú waited.

CHAPTER 20

Wolves

Leo opened his eyes slowly at the sound of his name. Blinking in the lamplight, he looked up into Gus's frightened face.

"Leo," she said urgently. She was standing over the mattress that Leo had been sleeping on. Her brown eyes were wide with panic. "You have to wake up!"

Leo sat up. "What?"

The window between the twin beds was wide open. A sharp breeze blew through, making the curtain that hung down over the window stand straight away from it. Ila's bed was quiet and still. Only Bear, looking forlorn and forgotten, sat on top of the rumpled coverlet.

"Where's Ila?" Leo said. "Gus, where's Ila?"

"I checked the bathroom," Gus answered, her voice tight and frightened. "And then I checked the kitchen—you know, in case she was hungry or something. And the living room. And everywhere. Leo, I checked everywhere! She's gone."

"No," Leo said, jumping up and frantically pulling the blankets off of Ila's bed, as though she might somehow be hiding among them.

"Get the Mórai," Gus said. "I'll search the house again."

Ila was not in the living room, or the kitchen, or the small bathroom. Back in the bedroom, looking under the beds, Gus heard Leo in the living room. She found him shutting all of the windows.

"Help me," he said. He told her that he'd found the Mórai in the lighthouse, in the small keeper's room. "She said to come back here and to lock all the windows and then go to your room and shut the door and wait there."

The twins quickly did as they had been told. Leo went into his room and got dressed while Gus pulled on her blue jeans and a sweater. When Leo knocked, she let him in and shut the door behind him. They sat on Ila's empty bed, waiting.

"Do you think it was the wolves?" Gus burst out.

"No," Leo said quickly. "Remember, the Mórai said we were safe here. And I haven't seen any prints, have you?"

Gus shook her head. A fresh wave of fear swept over her, and with it, a new and awful suspicion. What if Ila had run away? Her eyes met Leo's. She could tell that he was thinking the same thing.

Just then, the door to their room burst open and the Mórai rushed in. Her previous exhaustion had faded.

"It's my fault!" Leo cried.

"What are you talking about?" Gus said. "Of course it's not your fault!"

"I fought with her over the stupid checkers game," Leo said miserably. "And then I teased her about the book, about not being able to read. And then, when we Turned . . ."

Tears filled Gus's eyes. Of course it was their fault. They had left Ila behind to Turn, and now she had left them.

The Móraí sat down on Gus's bed. "It's not your fault," she said to them. "It is mine. She has not simply run away. She has left with someone she trusts. The Bedell is gone as well."

"Maybe he came to get her to let her Turn," Gus said. "You know, because she was so mad before, when she didn't get to Turn with us." The thought made her fear soften a bit at its edges.

But the Móraí was shaking her head. "He has taken the skidbladnin. There is no reason to take the boat unless he has a journey in mind. I fear he has taken your sister to the Dobhar-chú."

"No!" Gus gasped. It didn't make any sense. "The Bedell is on our side," she said, blushing at how silly it sounded.

But Leo was nodding. "He's helping us," he agreed. "Why would he take Ila?"

The Móraí looked very sad. "When I made the Bedell my Messenger, I saved his life. But what kind of life did I give him? The last of his kind, alone on an island with an old woman for company. I should have allowed him to pass away as the other sea minks had done. Instead, I made him the loneliest creature in existence."

"But he loves Ila," Leo said.

The Móraí nodded. "He does. But the Dobhar-chú must have promised him something that would overcome the love he bears for Ila."

An image came to Gus then, of the Bedell being sent from the table so that the true Folk could speak in private. She knew, without a doubt, what the little man might want badly enough to betray the children that he was charged to protect.

"His family," Leo said, speaking Gus's thoughts. "He's bringing back the sea minks."

"Can the Dobhar-chú do that?" Gus asked. "Bring them back from the dead?"

The Móraí shook her head. "He cannot. But the Bedell does not know that. He thinks he is getting his family back, but I'm afraid he is only getting death, once the Dobhar-chú is done with him."

"Where are they?" Gus said. "How do we get there? When do we leave?"

"Now," the Móraí said. "I'd hoped to take more time to train you two, now that you are eleven, but I'm afraid we are out of time."

Even as she spoke, a noise came from below the house. It sounded like a huge wailing creature, something out of dark stories rising from the sea. It was the wolves, howling as they swam to the island.

"I am sorry," the Móraí said. "I am so sorry, children. They are here."

The front door blew open, slamming against the wall, and then the little house filled with the sound of the Dobhar-chú's wolves, like a hurricane come to tear the house to shreds.

"To the beach!" the Móraí shouted.

Leo pushed open the closed window and leapt through it. Gus followed, climbing awkwardly through the small opening and landing on her hands and knees outside. The Móraí came last, falling to the ground with a cry. Leo helped her up and she stood for a moment, her hands on her knees. "Come," she finally said, lifting her head. "We must hurry."

They scrambled straight down below the lighthouse, navigating around the rocks that the Móraí had warned them to avoid. Below them, the waves hissed and crashed and broke with hollow booms. The Móraí moved slowly but surely across the slick rocks. Behind her, Gus and Leo slid and fell to keep up. When they finally stopped, Gus's hands were bleeding and her jeans had ripped where she had fallen on one knee.

Morning was just breaking over the sea with a steely, sunless light. They were standing in a shallow cave, more of an impression, really, in the sheer rock face. In front of them, waves rolled and broke on the jagged rocks that ringed the entrance to the cave. It wasn't much of a shelter, and they were quickly soaked through by the salty spray of the breaking waves.

The Mórai turned to where Gus and Leo huddled against the rock. She spoke quietly, but somehow they could hear her over the crashing surf. "I did not mean for it to be like this." Her face creased slightly, as though a pain had passed through her body, but she shook her head and kept speaking, quietly but urgently.

"You must go after Ila. You will find that it is easy to track her, once you are in your true forms. When you find her, wait for me. You must not fight the Dobhar-chú alone. Together we can defeat him, but none of us is strong enough to do it on our own."

Gus nodded, but Leo thought back to what he had read in the book. Whoever killed the Dobhar-chú would also die. The Mórai was going to sacrifice herself for them.

"But you can't," he began to say.

The Mórai cut off his protest with a quick, sharp shake of her head. "I will hold back the wolves. I can buy you some time, but not much. I will come as soon as I am able."

She bent down and held Gus's face between her hands. She looked into Gus's eyes, and then, without any warning, she kissed Gus on the forehead. Then she did the same to Leo.

"Now, quickly, take hands."

Gus squeezed Leo's hand as hard as she could. Her face was soaked with salt water and she could barely see the Mórai through the spray that was all around them. She could feel her heart pounding in her chest. *Think of Ila,* she told herself. *Nothing else.*

"I'm ready," she said.

"I'm ready too," Leo said beside her.

A chorus of howls rent the air above their heads.

"Now," the Mórai called. "Lost Children, come!"

Gus and Leo were plunged into darkness.

They could feel their hearts beating, and their fingers gripping each other's, but they could neither see, nor hear, nor smell anything at all. It was the darkness of a star waiting to be born, without light, or heat, or sound, or motion to propel it or to hold it still. Just nothing, everywhere, pressing in on them, filling them with nothing and nowhere and endless and forever.

They suddenly heard seals calling wildly, from far away, and behind that the dimmer howling of wolves, but then a rushing forward propelled them and they heard, beyond the seals and the wolves and the crash of the sea, the sound of stars calling to them like distant wind and music wound together. Throwing back their heads, Gus and Leo answered the stars, releasing their grips on one another's hands to open their arms wide, and wider, and wider still to the wild water and the waiting skies.

The two seals moved instinctively forward, toward the comfort of the sea. Once in the water, they surfaced and looked at the beach. The Mórai stood with her back to them. Her arms were stretched over her head and her long white hair was plastered to her body by the wind that whipped around her like a miniature tornado. The wolves, reaching the beach, crouched low in a ring around the old woman, biding their time, choosing their moment to leap.

Her words came faintly to them on the ragged, blowing sea wind. "Swim," she was shouting. "Swim!"

The seals dove in unison. Soon they were alone in the dark water that the light could not reach. They evened out then, and sped forward for a while until they had to breathe.

Gus torqued her powerful body and shot upward, racing faster and faster to the surface and then bursting out with an enormous exhalation of spent air, *woofing* and looking around as she did so. A second sleek head broke the surface next to her.

They hung in the water side by side for a minute, basking in the joy of being in the sea in these bodies again. Then they began to search for Ila. Seals do not have good vision on land, but below the water's surface their large round eyes can pick out details that humans could never hope to see. So they began by looking, diving and circling and peering into the murk for any sign of a swimming fox or a little seal. When that search turned up nothing, they tried listening, and finally smelling the water for any traces. They found nothing.

Then, without thinking much about it, Gus began to

move her upper lip back and forth as she swam, feeling with the stiff whiskers on her muzzle for any disturbances in the water. Almost immediately, she sensed several vibrations. One, a light, flicking sense of motion, was a school of fish darting somewhere out in front of her. Another, more sonorous vibration was too ponderous to be anything but a right whale, slowly cruising the shallows for its favorite plankton.

But then her sensitive whiskers picked up something else, a vibration that was neither fish nor mammal. If it had a been a color, she would have described it as golden—a golden thread sparkling in the Atlantic as it stretched from Loup Marin behind them to the deeper water and beyond. Gus knew, without a doubt, that what she was sensing was the passing of the Bedell's magical gnome-made boat, the skidbladnin. She turned to Leo, who hung in the dark water beside her. He nodded his head once and they fell into formation, Leo just behind Gus, their whiskers trembling as they caught hold of the tenuous quivering sensation that would lead them to Ila.

The invisible thread took them forward effortlessly. Soon Loup Marin, the wolves, and the old woman who held them at bay so that the children could escape were nothing but a memory in their fast-moving wake, fading behind them in the sweet wind and distant cries of gulls, far up in the unbroken blue sky.

CHAPTER 21

A Wall of Fog

As Gus and Leo traveled under the surface of the sea, they discovered that they could communicate with one another. To their human ears, it might have sounded like the high-pitched squeals, tweets, and whistles of a radio searching for a station. But to their seal ears, it was language. When they had first Turned, with the Bedell's help, they had been too dazzled by their new forms to think about speaking. But this time, they were more comfortable. They could move without thinking, and take in the vast sensory input of the sea without being overwhelmed.

"More slow you!" Leo cheeped to Gus, who slowed down without realizing at first that Leo had spoken to her, and that she had understood it.

"Speak?" she chirped.

Leo came back with a burst of chirps and static that meant, broadly, "Yes. This is how we talk in these bodies."

He wasn't exactly saying that, of course. The seal

language seemed to be much more general than human speech. It did not, for example, include either past tense or future tense. When Gus tried to ask Leo how long he thought they had been swimming, the best she could do was "Swim long or short?"

But it worked. They could communicate.

They swam side by side for a while, practicing their new speech. Their bodies knew the language, even as they groped for words.

As they tuned into one another, they realized that they could hear other creatures speaking as well. There was the light chatter of fish (who talked only about food, food, and food). There was also the heavier, cello-like singing of a passing pod of killer whales. Their language was far more complicated than the seals', and Gus and Leo had trouble understanding it. They appeared to be arguing about the density of water as it related to its coloration, but neither seal could be sure.

They never saw the whales, which was just as well. If Leo had found the words for it, he would have told Gus that killer whales are called apex predators. That means that nothing hunts the killer whale, and it hunts everything. Leo struggled to convey this information, but the best he could come up with was a series of clicks and squeaks that meant something like "Danger, all kill not us, yes?"

Gus understood what he meant, and the two seals swam faster. Gradually, the killer whales and their debate faded, to be replaced by the clicking and yapping of dolphins, the low groans of tuna, and the constant chatter of the smaller fishes. The ocean could be quite a noisy place, Gus and Leo were discovering.

But then, quite suddenly, the sea around them fell silent. The chattering and singing and even the light chirps of the smallest fish stopped abruptly. A school of haddock dashed by, going the other way, their silvery bodies like hurrying ghosts in the water.

The vibration that was the passing of the skidbladnin stopped abruptly. In front of them was a wall of fog. Not the usual kind of fog, which sat just above the water or, occasionally, touched its surface, where it immediately broke into the water droplets that formed it. This fog was somehow keeping its shape *in* the water, extending as far down as either seal could see.

Gus and Leo hung in the strangely silent sea for a moment, looking at the fog. They knew what it was—the Folk's fog that kept the Dobhar-chú trapped on his island prison. And its existence meant that the Móraí was still alive.

With this fact buoying their spirits, the seals swam to the surface to breathe. From there, they could see that the fog hung like a curtain, completely hiding what might be behind it. The seals grabbed great lungfuls of air and then, with a nod to one another, they dove.

The fog-filled water felt thick and cold, even to their insulated seal bodies. They could feel no motion, and no wakes from the moving bodies of fish. The utter emptiness of the water was frightening. They swam slowly, so close together that their flippers brushed as they moved.

They came out of the fogbank side by side to find themselves in dark water. Then, suddenly, Gus's whiskers picked up a shape. A large shape, moving fast. It was far bigger than either of the seals and it seemed to be coming in their direction. Gus risked a slight chirp to Leo, who acknowledged her sudden fear. He had felt it too. Instinctively, the two seals hung totally still in the water, waiting to see what other information they could gather. That was when the great white shark exploded past them.

It was their stillness that saved their lives. Sharks can sense the changes in water pressure that happen when a fish thrashes around. Luckily for Gus and Leo, they had been still, and the shark's first rush took it past them. They could see its sleek form, overslung jaw, and one small black eye as it passed. Without thinking, communicating, or hesitating, the two seals dove and swam.

What also saved their lives was how little distance they had come. They tore through the fogbank and into the open sea before the great white could attack again. The shark was right behind them, but when it got to the inner edge of the fog, it slammed to a halt as if hitting a brick wall.

Sharks don't communicate with sound, but Gus and Leo both heard the giant creature thrashing in frustration. The two seals surfaced for great gulps of air after their panicked flight from the gray monster.

They hung there, peering into the fog with their weak above-water vision. Nothing moved, but when Gus put her muzzle back in the water and felt around, she could feel many shapes shifting restlessly on the inner side of the fogbank. The Dobhar-chú, it seemed, was not alone in his island prison. Some of the creatures who had fought with him also shared his punishment. Leo remembered the monsters in *The Book of the Folk*. Was there a giant blue squid swimming beyond the fog?

Gus's and Leo's seal bodies were made for motion, not strategy. It was almost impossible to think, as seals, about the future. The present moment was just too overwhelming. The smells and sounds of the sea flooded them, even as they tried to consider how they might get past the creatures beyond the fog.

"Fast, me!" Gus barked. "I swim first, and, and . . ." She stopped, frustrated. What she was trying to say was *I'll go first and distract the sharks and then you follow while they are chasing me,* but her seal body would not allow her to speak in such detail.

Leo understood enough to disagree. "No!" he barked. Then he dove.

Gus followed him, thinking that he might be planning something foolish. But Leo was hanging in the water just below the surface.

"I call help," Leo said in the underwater language of the seals.

Gus was puzzled. Call whom? How? There was no word for *book* in the seal language, so Leo could not tell

Gus that he had read in *The Book of the Folk* how the Folk called on the other creatures of the sea to come and aid them in their fight against the Dobhar-chú. He could only show her. So he began to sing.

At first, the sound was halting and hesitant, as Leo struggled to remember the exact sequence of notes that he had read about in the book. But when his voice gained power, rising through the water in a twisting, haunting tune without words, Gus realized that she recognized the music. It was the song that had come out of *The Book of the Folk* when the Móraí had shown it to them. She closed her eyes as Leo sang, listening as the tune moved through the water in waves, spreading out and around the two seals like ripples in a still pond.

Leo sang the song through twice, and then one more time. As he neared the end of the third round, his voice quieted, and then faded away.

They hung there for a moment, just breathing.

"Beautiful," Gus said to Leo.

"Yes," he said.

They waited for a long time. The peace that had flooded their bodies as Leo sang began to seep away as the water around them stayed flat and still and empty. Finally, Gus spoke.

"No one," she said. "We go."

"Scared," Leo said.

"Yes," said Gus.

They decided that Gus would enter the fog first and distract the creature who patrolled its boundary. Then

Leo would slip in behind her and make for the island. Gus would follow Leo as soon as she could.

"Get Ila," Gus said.

The two seals pressed their muzzles together briefly.

"Safe," Leo said.

"Fast," Gus said, and turned and swam for the wall of fog.

Leo swept his whiskers through the water one last time, looking for any kind of vibration at all to tell him that help was coming. When he felt nothing, he turned and, with a heart full of dread, followed his sister.

Gus knew what she had to do. The shark they had seen could not pass through the fog, so if she could stay close to its inner edge, she should be able to give Leo a chance to make for the island. In theory, she could pop in and out of the fog and evade her pursuer. But she had no idea if it would work. She was terribly, terribly frightened. She reminded herself that she was the fastest swimmer in the school. This form was meant for speed in the water. She could do this. She *had* to do this. Ila was depending on them. Their mother was depending on them. Gus took a deep breath at the surface, barked once at Leo, and dove.

The plan went wrong almost immediately. As soon as Gus was in the fog, she lost Leo. He was supposed to be right behind her, but she could not feel him there. She put out a questioning trill, but there was no answer. Then all thought of Leo was driven from Gus's head because she popped out of the fog and was immediately surrounded by the overlapping wakes of sharks. Not one shark but a crowd. The ripples from their moving bodies overwhelmed Gus's sensitive whiskers. She froze, trying to be invisible. It worked for about five seconds. Then the sharks, all at once, charged.

Gus spun, dove, and shot out through the fog into the clear water. She could hear the frantic thrashing of the angry sharks behind her. Leo was still at the edge of the fog.

"Move," Gus said angrily to him.

"Bad idea!"

"Only idea!" Gus trilled back at him. Her heart was pounding with terror, and she knew that if she didn't go back into the fog right now, she never would. So, leaping forward in the water, Gus shoved Leo into the fog. He bellowed angrily at her, and she gave him a sharp bite on his flank. As he shot forward into the misty water, she followed him.

The sharks were waiting on the other side.

"Go left!" Gus called, and then she shot right, toward the mass of gray bodies, her heart pounding, her only hope that Leo would listen to her and get to the island. Just before the pack overtook her, she sensed Leo moving away off to her left and felt a great rush of relief. Then the pack was on her and she dove and twisted and swam.

Gus swam faster than she ever had in her life. Even as terror threatened to overcome her, part of her gloried in the feeling. This was what she was good at. This was what she could do, better and faster than anyone else she knew. And perhaps better and faster than anyone in the sea. She rocketed through the water with the sharks at her back. She dodged and rolled and lunged through the fog into the open ocean, and then through the fog again into the shark-filled water, infuriating the pursuing beasts. They chased her in a frenzy, like a pack of dogs pursuing a fox who continually outwits them.

An iridescent mako shark snapped at Gus with its pointed muzzle. As she rolled out of the reach of the mako, Gus felt the ripple in the water from another shark's snapping jaws, much too close. She dove through the curtain of fog, caught her breath, and swam back in. Another mako charged her, and her dodge sent her into a tailspin through the water. Dizzy and confused, she briefly closed her eyes to orient herself and then re-opened them to see the gaping maw of the shark as it lunged for her. With a final burst of strength, Gus spun away from the mako—and directly into the massive bulk of a charging bull shark. Luckily, it was expecting her to move away from, not toward it, and so its attack went wide, but its gaping jaws caught her left flipper as it barreled past. Gus screamed in terror and pain as a thin ribbon of her blood drifted through the water.

But for some reason, even as her flipper bled into the sea, the sharks did not attack again. Instead, they began to bump her with their bodies, driving her forward, like dogs herding a sheep. A tiger shark, young enough that its stripes had not yet faded, slammed up against Gus, sending her careening helplessly through the water. As she found her balance and tried to flee, the bull shark who had charged her earlier slammed his stout body against hers, making her ears ring and her vision go dark.

They were playing with her, she realized. They could have killed her easily by now, and yet they were merely bumping and jostling her. Then, without warning, the sharks stopped. They hung in the water, surrounding her but not coming any closer. For a wild moment, Gus thought they were going to let her go. Her sensitive whiskers, picking up the new vibration in the water, told her otherwise. The great white was coming.

Gus turned for the fog, and saw with a stab of terror that the sharks had been herding her away from the fog curtain. Because of her injured flipper, she had been swimming slightly to the left. The sharks had taken advantage of her handicap, and had herded her in that direction. Now the safety of the fog wall hung at least five hundred yards away. Much too far to outrun a hunting great white.

Leo, Gus thought to herself. *Maybe Leo got through.* Then, with her injured flipper tucked in against her body, she turned to face the approaching monster.

Suddenly the water around Gus exploded. One minute she was hanging motionless, surrounded by waiting sharks, and the next, the water was alive with twisting silvery bodies and the chattering, yammering cries of hunting dolphins. One rammed the tiger shark nearest Gus and sent it spinning off into the deep water. The dolphin twittered a greeting at Gus and then butted a mako, flipping it end over end.

A larger body whooshed by Gus, and then another, and another. Gus saw the flash of white bellies on sleek black bodies as the creatures filled the sea around her. It was the pod of killer whales that she and Leo had heard earlier. Their cello-like singing was gone. They moved with total silence through the water, plowing through the sharks, scattering them right and left. Their target, though, was the great white. It came up through the water like a torpedo, its jaws wide, and was met by the killers. Killer whales fight like wolves, in packs, and it was a pack that descended on the great white. At least a dozen sets of jaws closed on the monster, pulling it down to the depths as they rolled it over, keeping it from defending itself. The cries of the dolphins filled the water as blood turned the sea pink. Gus was frozen with shock. One of the dolphins swam to her.

"Go! Go! Go!" it squeaked, giving Gus a sharp nudge with its beak for emphasis. A tiger shark exploded out of the water next to the dolphin, who turned with a shrill scream to meet it.

Gus needed no more encouragement. Holding her injured flipper close to her side, she shot through the water using only her body and powerful tail. She slipped by the battle unnoticed and made for the island, where she hoped Leo and Ila were waiting.

Waves carried her the final few yards. One wave threw her exhausted body up against a rocky shoreline and then pulled her back out again. The next time a wave caught her, she rallied her strength and flopped out of the water and onto a long, low rock. She tried to move toward the shore, but the adrenaline abruptly left her bloodstream, and shaking and nauseous, she collapsed.

A small, dark seal moved awkwardly down the rock toward her, barking anxiously. It was Leo. Gus tried to answer, but she was too exhausted. She closed her eyes as the seal reached her. After a few minutes of anxious watching, Leo stretched out next to his sister. Resting his neck across her back, he closed his eyes. They had a long way to go, but for now they were alive, and it was good enough.

CHAPTER 22

Help from the Sea

A wave breaking over them startled both seals into wakefulness. It was late afternoon and the slanting sun was warm, but then another wave crashed, washing them into the water.

They swam back and forth in the whitewater, searching for a way to access the island. Finally, Leo stopped in front of an outcropping of granite that had been worn by the waves into a series of blocky steps. Seals could not climb up them, but humans could. They Turned and climbed up the wet, cold rock as quickly as they could, shivering in the suddenly freezing water.

The top was wet, but at least it was out of range of the crashing waves. They sat there for a few minutes, letting the sun warm them. Leo was wearing his glasses.

"Isn't it weird that we end up in our clothes?" Leo finally said. "Like, shouldn't we—"

"Shh," Gus said waving a hand at him. "Ow!" Moving

her left arm sent a bolt of pain all the way down to her fingers.

"What happened?" Leo said anxiously. "Gus, you're bleeding!"

Gus put her right hand up to her left arm. Just below the shoulder, her shirt was ripped. The skin under the shredded material was torn and bleeding.

"I'm OK," she said. "It's just a bite."

Leo's eyes bulged and Gus couldn't help laughing, even though her arm *did* hurt like crazy. "Just a shark bite," she repeated, feeling slightly hysterical.

"Wow," Leo said, looking at her with something like awe.

"Can you take a look at it?" Gus said.

Leo pulled away the cloth and peered at Gus's arm. "Actually, it's not that bad," he said with obvious relief. "It's sort of ripped up a little bit, but the bleeding's pretty much stopped. Not bad for a shark bite."

Gus grinned at him.

Leo tore off the rest of Gus's sleeve, and after leaning over to soak the material in the sea, he tied it around her arm as a makeshift bandage.

"That should do it," he said cheerfully, tying off the flowered cloth.

"How did you know that song?" Gus asked.

Leo blushed. "I sort of snuck out and read the book some more," he admitted.

"What else did you find out?" Gus demanded. "And why didn't you tell me?"

"I knew you'd be mad," Leo said, knowing as he spoke how weak an excuse it was. "And there wasn't really time. You and Ila were gone all day, and then . . ."

His voice trailed off. *And then Ila was taken* was what he'd been going to say.

"Anyway," Gus said quickly. "What else did you learn?"

Leo shoved his glasses up on his nose. "Well, about the battle, and the way that the Folk called for help and— By the way," he interrupted himself, "you didn't see a giant blue squid in there, did you?" he indicated the ocean with his head. "Or an orange dragon thingy?"

"Just sharks," Gus said.

"Well, that's good, anyway," Leo said. "That must mean the other creatures were all killed off by the Folk."

"Maybe," Gus said. "Or maybe they just don't like sharks."

"Gus," Leo said hesitantly. "I also read something else." He told her about the curse that killing the King of the Black Lakes carried. "That's why the Mórai said to wait for her," he explained. "So she can be the one who kills him."

"She's going to sacrifice herself," Gus said. Tears rose up in her eyes, but all she said was "I wish we'd known her sooner."

"I do too," Leo said.

They were both silent for a minute, watching the waves crashing and boiling below them. A particularly large one sprayed them with a fine mist. Farther out the fog hung steady and thick, blocking their view of the horizon.

Then Gus turned to look at the island, and Leo followed her gaze. Jagged granite climbed up from the water as far as they could see. If Loup Marin was a pile of rocks, this nameless island was more like a boulder field sprawled out at the base of steep, craggy cliffs. The rocks, which ranged in size from scattered chunks of granite to boulders as tall as several stacked cars, were dull gray and reddish brown, sparked here and there with shining bits of quartz. It looked as though a giant's castle had collapsed and the island was its ruins.

At the very tops of the cliffs, they could just see pine trees.

"How are we ever going to get up there?" Gus said.

They scrambled and crawled and pulled themselves up and over for a while, trying to find a way to the cliffs. Gus's fingers on her right hand were bleeding from scraping across the rough granite. Her left arm was mostly useless. At one point, Leo slipped and slid all the way back down to the shoreline, ripping the knees of his jeans and landing hard at the bottom.

"We're not really getting anywhere," Gus panted as Leo hauled her up and over another rock. She was right. As a wave crashed by their feet, spraying them with cold salt water, they realized that they were actually closer to the water than they had been before. They had moved sideways a few hundred feet, but that was it.

"Well, there isn't really—" Leo started to say, but he was interrupted by a sound rising from somewhere amid the rocks. It was a wolf, howling. The first howl was answered almost immediately by a series of other howls. They seemed to be coming from slightly above Gus and Leo.

They looked at each other in horror.

"Lie down," Leo hissed.

Flat against the rock, they turned their heads and looked in the direction that the sound had come from.

There, standing above the broken chunks of wet rock that they had used to climb out of the water, was a gray wolf. The wolf was tall but skinny, almost gaunt, and when it turned toward where the children lay, they could see that its eyes were an unnatural, burning red.

The wolf looked in their direction for one endless minute, and then it turned back to the other wolves, who were trotting down through the boulder field in single file. They didn't appear to be hunting just yet. They were gathering. More and more gray bodies slipped like ghosts between the boulders to join the wolf who had called them.

"There must be more than a hundred of them," Leo whispered in Gus's ear. As he spoke, one of the wolves tilted its great, bony head toward them. Curling its lip, it snarled deep and low in its chest. Instantly the milling wolves froze.

Gus could barely breathe. She was more frightened than she had ever been in her life, even more than she had been in the water with the sharks. In the water, she had her speed. Out here on land, she and Leo were trapped. There was nowhere to go. Leo squeezed her hand, once, twice, three times. Not daring to turn her head, she peeked at him out of the corner of one eye.

"Climb," he mouthed. She squeezed his hand back to let him know that she understood. The wolves stood between them and the water. Their only hope was to find a way up one of the cliffs.

They slipped to the ground and began to pick their way toward the nearest cliff face. Trying to stay low, they ducked into a short tunnel formed by two steep-sided boulders. But the tunnel ran out where the two boulders met. It was a dead end.

"This way," Gus said urgently. Putting her back against one wall of rock, she placed both of her feet flat on the other side. By hitching up her backside and then moving her feet, she was able to inch her way up through the tight space. Leo followed her lead, and when they reached the top they could see a rough wall nearby, cut with cracks and fissures and very high. It was their only chance.

"Run for it," Leo said.

As he spoke, a howl broke loose behind them. One

of the wolves had found a way through and was signaling to her pack mates.

"Run!" Leo screamed, and he and Gus leapt to the ground and began to sprint.

They could hear a wolf in the tunnel. It was whining and growling, trying to find a way to follow the twins' scent trail. It scratched at the sides of the short tunnel, but it could not climb out the way that Gus and Leo had.

Gus and Leo reached the wall and scanned it desperately for any features that might help them climb. The rock was broken with cracks, but they all seemed to run horizontally across the face, not vertically.

"There," Gus said, pointing at one narrow crack that ran up the dark face. "Boost me."

Leo clasped his hands and Gus stepped up and onto the cliff face. Reaching high, she stuck the fingers of her right hand into a horizontal crack. Then she jammed her sneaker sideways into the vertical crack, the way their father had taught them when he took them rock climbing in the Camden Hills. Then she had been wearing a harness and sticky shoes. Now she had only her fear, but it was enough. Pressing down with her sweaty, slippery fingers, she turned her foot and stood on it. The pain made her gasp, but her foot held. Below her, Leo started to climb.

"Keep going," he said through gritted teeth as he stuck his own foot into the crack.

Gus jammed her other foot above the first one in the crack and stood up on that, and then repeated the series of steps. Leo was just below her. Gus leaned back and looked up. One of the horizontal cracks over her head formed a very small ledge. If she could move her foot up again, she might be able to reach the ledge with her hands.

Suddenly Leo screamed. He had one foot in the crack and his fingers on the wall, clutching at slight bumps in the rock. The other foot was kicking at a gigantic, red-eyed, slathering wolf crouched below him.

"Leo!" Gus screamed as the wolf leapt.

Leo kicked and his sneaker connected with the wolf's jaw, snapping it back. The animal fell to the ground, snarling horribly. Leo scrambled up another few inches on the wall, and then another. His head bumped into Gus's lower foot.

"Move, Gus!" he shouted.

The wolf on the ground leapt for Leo, and leapt again, each time falling short. Without hesitating or even thinking about it, Gus stepped up high and jammed her foot into the crack. She twisted it to lock it in place, stood up, and lunged for the tiny ledge above her head. In her fear, she forgot the pain of her injured arm. Her hands slapped the rough granite and slid, and then her fingers found the lip of the ledge and held. She stood with the side of her face pressed against the cool stone, trembling. She could sense her brother moving up the rock just below her.

"Leo," she said, his name coming out as a sob.

"I'm OK," Leo said.

Gus looked down at him. He had both his feet and both his hands in the crack and was breathing heavily. His eyes were huge and his hair looked very black against his paper-white face.

Gus took a deep breath and tried to relax her fingers, which were starting to cramp. "I'm OK too," she said. She took another deep breath.

Now the other wolves were gathering below them, pressing into the small space between the rocks, snarling and snapping and leaping. Each leap fell short, though. Gus and Leo were safe, for the moment.

"Can you climb any higher?" Leo asked, raising his voice over the noise of the increasingly furious wolves.

Gus looked up. The crack ran out at the ledge. Beyond that the wall was smooth and unmarked. "No," she said. "I can't go any farther, Leo."

She tried to keep the panic out of her voice. She knew that they could not stay like this much longer. Already her feet were aching from being jammed in the crack, but worse, her cramped fingers were now going numb.

"We'll wait them out, Gus!" Leo said.

Gus nodded, even though she knew they could not wait out the wolves. There were easily a hundred wolves below them now, some leaping, some resting between efforts, and some looking for another way to reach the twins. She pressed her forehead against the rock. Hot tears streaked down her face, not from the pain in her foot, although it was fierce, and not even from the terrible fear that was filling her entire body. She was crying because they had failed Ila. And now Ila was going to die, and their mother as well. The Móraí had put her faith in them and they had failed her.

Gus leaned into the rock and sobbed. She was crying so hard that she didn't notice that the wolves had gone quiet.

"Gus!" Leo shouted. "Gus!"

Gus looked down at Leo. He was looking down as well, at the wolves, who had stopped snarling and howling. They were milling around uncertainly. One small female sniffed the air anxiously and whined.

"What is it?" Gus asked hoarsely.

"Something's weird," Leo said. "They can tell."

Two more wolves started whining, tucking their tails between their legs and crouching down like frightened dogs.

"Gus," Leo said in a careful, low voice. "Gus? Look at the ocean."

Gus peered over one shoulder toward the water. What she saw did not make any sense. Just inside the fog boundary, a series of mountains had sprung up in the sea. Then one of the mountains moved and she realized that it was a whale. It was *a lot* of whales, stretched side by side as far as she could see from her awkward position.

"No dorsal fin," Leo said excitedly. "That means they're right whales, Gus!"

Below him, a wolf suddenly let loose a long, thin, uneasy-sounding howl. The wolf next to it shuddered and then joined in.

"Why does it matter what kind of whales they are?" Gus steadied herself and then let one hand dangle for a moment, getting the blood flowing back into her fingers.

"Because right whales love to lobtail," Leo said as if it were the most obvious thing in the world.

"What—" Gus began, but Leo interrupted her.

"Hang on, Gus!" he said. He hastily jammed one arm into the crack. "If they're going to lobtail, then we really, really need to hang on!"

"Have you gone totally crazy?" Gus said angrily. "What's lobtailing, and how is it going to help us?"

But even as she spoke, the great black lumps in the ocean dove as one. And then, also as one, fifty whales' tails, with their smooth, pointed flukes spread wide above the water, hovered for exactly three seconds and then slapped down with one hundred tons of force per whale.

"Lobtailing!" Leo shouted.

The whales raised their tails again, and again they slammed them against the water in unison, and then again, and again, each time forcing more energy into the water.

The fifth time the whales lobtailed, the energy building under the water burst up and out as a gigantic wave. The wave grew as it moved, gaining speed and height as it sped toward the rocky shoreline, like a freight train barreling down a mountainside. When it hit the rocks, instead of disintegrating, the giant wave grew still taller as all of its energy was forced upward by the impact. It kept coming, higher than a house, dense and black and screaming with energy. The wolves below Gus and Leo were screaming as well, their mouths open in terror and the fur standing up along their narrow backs. A few tried to leap onto the rocks, but most of them just ran in a blind panic, tripping and howling and bumping into each other as the enormous wave crested the beach.

"Turn!" Leo screamed, and then the wave hit.

The water tore Gus and Leo off the wall as though they were made of straw. They were flipped upside down and flung backward, pitched into the maelstrom along with rocks and dirt and drowning wolves. Gus tried not to panic, but she couldn't get her bearings—there was no *up* in this lashing tornado of angry water. She curled herself into a tight ball, but she was immediately yanked out of it so that she pinwheeled frantically, thrashing her arms and legs as the water raged at her, flipping and tossing her helpless form in the heaving darkness. The burning in her lungs reached a screaming pitch, and she opened her mouth and swallowed as though it might be air, although of course it wasn't—it was burning salt water and she was choking, choking and kicking and everywhere was blackness.

Something bumped her, hard, and then she thought she felt the hairy body of a wolf pass over her, but she couldn't be sure and she was trying to remember what Leo had shouted as the wave hit, but she was so tired, and she couldn't think straight. Then she was shooting forward like a rocket, and *up* was easy because she could smell the surface and the flat scent of ozone, so different from the tang of the sea. She shot out of the confusion into the open ocean and gulped in a huge breath.

The sea was flat. The whales had gone, and it was as if they had folded up their wave and taken it with them. All around Gus floated the bodies of wolves, battered and drowned. She looked frantically for Leo but could see only driftwood and dead wolves. Then a sleek head surfaced and Gus barked loudly. Leo swam quickly to her.

The whales had saved them from the wolves, but they were still in danger. Even now, they could see sharp dorsal fins cutting the surface of the sea. The surviving sharks were coming, drawn by the smell of death. Without making a sound, the two seals swam to the rock that they had used as a staircase, Turned, and climbed up out of the water.

They could see the slight whirlpools left in the water as the wolves' floating bodies were yanked under by the arriving carnivores. Gus shuddered and looked away, toward the island. More wolves lay broken among the boulders. The whales' wave had done its work well.

"Thank you," Leo said quietly. Gus looked at him. He was facing out to sea. When he looked at her, she gasped. He was still wearing his glasses, but his wet hair was plastered to his head and a livid gash cut across his forehead. One of his eyes was swollen shut, and a great purple bruise spread below that eye and across his cheek-bone.

"You look terrible," Gus said.

Leo grinned. "You don't look so hot yourself," he said.

Gus surveyed herself. One leg of her blue jeans was ripped off below her knee. The flowered bandage was still tied tightly around the wound on her arm, but it was sodden with seawater. She had a dull ache in her side that twinged sharply when she moved, and a stinging scrape on the side of her face. But other than that, she seemed to be unhurt by the massive wave. She sat down, suddenly exhausted. Leo sat down next to her.

"You called the right whales?" Gus asked.

Leo grinned. "Yup. Well, I didn't know it would be *them*, exactly. I just called for help with the song. Right whales are pretty slow swimmers. I guess that's why they came after the others. Lucky for us, though."

He pushed his glasses up, looking suddenly like the old Leo. "They never lobtail in unison like that," he added excitedly. "Not ever. I'd love to see it again."

"No thanks," Gus said fervently. "And we're not dead, which is good, but we're still stuck on this beach."

"Oh!" Leo said. "I was thinking about that, you know, while we were on that wall. Remember when the wolves came?"

Gus shuddered. "Um, yeah."

"I mean *how* they came."

Gus looked at him blankly.

"Single file!" Leo said. "Remember? Wolves don't usually travel like that, unless, you know, they're in deep snow and trying to conserve energy. Then they'll often hunt in a single-file line—"

"So what, Leo?" Gus interrupted him. She was far too tired to appreciate the intricacies of the animal world.

"So I think they were on a path," Leo said. "There's no other explanation. They must have been following a trail of some sort."

It took a minute for Leo's words to sink into Gus's exhausted brain, but when they did, she felt a sudden burst of energy. She stood up and looked for a moment at the flat blue sea. Then, turning to face the island, she nodded at Leo, who jumped up to stand beside her.

"So," Gus said. "Let's find Ila."

CHAPTER 23

Traveling by Pool

Once they knew what they were looking for, it didn't take long. Leo was right. The wolves *had* followed a trail. Winding around the boulders was a thin, snaking path of paw prints and packed dirt barely wide enough for one person. It led them up the boulder field to the base of a craggy cliff. This cliff looked the same as the one they had tried to climb—blocky, reddish brown, cut by cracks, and furred in places with bright green lichen.

"The trail ends here," Leo said, peering down at the scuffed patch of dirt at the base of the crag.

"No," Gus said. "Look—the prints go behind the rock."

She was right. A flake of rock jutted out from the cliff. It was just possible to slip behind it. There, in the narrow space between the flake and the rock face, was a steep passageway. Without another word, Gus and Leo set off, scrabbling with their hands and feet to climb. The space between the rock face and the flake was dark, and damp, and spidery. Wet moss grew in clumps on the rocks on either side of them. Several times the space became so narrow that they were forced to turn sideways and inch along awkwardly. They crawled up the last bit and found themselves, muddy and exhausted, gazing at the dark, fibrous roots of pine trees.

Leo pulled himself up and over the edge of the crag by grabbing the trees' roots. Then he bent down and helped Gus, whose left arm was beginning to throb painfully again.

"Can you see the path?" Gus asked. She wiped her one remaining sleeve across her sweaty, grimy face. She could taste dirt in her mouth, which reminded her how thirsty she was.

Leo nodded. He was filthy too; mud was caked under his fingernails and the legs of his jeans were sodden. "I think so. Look up ahead."

He pointed to the scruffy pine trees that had dug their scrubby roots into bits of soil and cracks in the rock. "See—in there. You can just see a few tracks."

They stood for one more minute at the edge of the wood. Looking behind them, they saw the ocean, now far below, throwing itself onto the rocky beach. The sun was low and the water was bitterly dark.

"Let's go," Gus said, trying to sound brave. The woods looked as chilly and unwelcoming as the evening sea. But there was a trail, no matter how faint, and it just might lead them to Ila. Taking a deep breath, Gus stepped into the woods, with Leo right behind her.

The winding track led them deeper and deeper into the woods. They were soon covered with thin scratches from the trees, which seemed to push in on them as they walked. There was no breeze in the forest, no rustling of leaves or scurrying of animals. The only sounds were their feet crunching on small twigs and the noises the branches made as they shoved at them. Gus looked back just once. All she could see were the heavy shapes of pine trees. Limbs blocked the way they had come.

Suddenly Gus stopped walking. "I can't see the trail," she said.

Leo knelt down and peered at the dirt. "Maybe that way?" he said, sounding uncertain.

"It's too dark," Gus said. "We need to stop. And we need to sleep." She would have liked to eat as well, but there was no sense in mentioning that. Food would just have to wait.

"Let's walk off a bit," Leo suggested.

For a few minutes, they moved away from where they thought the path was. Leo found a large boulder that formed an overhang where the soil had been worn away.

"Perfect," he said happily. "And look—water!"

One side of the boulder was covered in moss, and a thin trickle of water ran through the moss to gather in a pool at the base of the rock.

"Do you think it's clean?" Gus said hesitantly. Leo put his face against the rock and lapped at the water like a cat trying to drink from a fountain.

"It tastes good," he announced.

It tasted *great*. Gus and Leo took turns sipping the water, and when they were done drinking, they splashed their grimy faces and Leo cleaned the cut on his forehead. Then, feeling immeasurably more optimistic, they broke off armfuls of pine branches to make beds.

"Tomorrow we'll find Ila, right?" Gus said as she slid under the overhanging rock onto her nest of pine branches. The space was cramped, but it was dry and much warmer than the open nighttime forest.

Leo murmured sleepily, something about Folk, and the book.

"What?" Gus asked him, but the only answer she got was even breathing. He was asleep already.

Sighing, she turned on her side and pulled her knees up to her chest for more warmth. It didn't seem possible that she could fall asleep. Images kept passing behind her closed eyelids—charging sharks, and snarling wolves, and great whales lining up in the ocean . . . The images faded to the dark blue of the deep water, and then to black. When Gus opened her eyes again, sunlight was streaming into their little space, and Leo was gone.

Gus sat up in a panic, banging her head on the low roof. Rubbing the smarting spot, she slid out of the space and jumped to her feet, scanning the forest for Leo. She pulled on her sneakers and ran in the direction she thought they had come from, calling his name, all thoughts of being quiet forgotten. As she burst out of the underbrush, she nearly collided with her brother. He was standing on the wolves' path, and he looked different. He was clean, Gus realized. Shining clean. He grinned at her from under a wet mop of hair.

"I found a pool," he said.

While they walked, Leo spoke over his shoulder.

"I was trying to follow the trail, but I got off it somehow. And so I was looking all around for paw prints, and I didn't find any, but I found this instead—look!"

He stopped suddenly and bent down in front of a red spruce. Its drooping lower branches, covered in bright green lichen, brushed the ground. Leo pulled aside some of the branches to reveal a perfectly round pool, big enough for three or maybe four people to sit in at one time. The water was clear and fresh and smelled like—

"Salt?" Gus said in disbelief. She bent down, stuck her finger in the pool, and licked it. It was salty.

"That's so weird," she said. "How could there be a saltwater pool here?"

"It must connect somehow to the ocean," Leo said reasonably.

"But how?" Gus said. "I don't see a stream leading to it, do you?"

"No," Leo admitted. "I couldn't find one either."

Just then, a silvery fish darted across the pool. Gus's stomach rumbled loudly. Hunger attacked her insides, biting and twisting at the emptiness in her.

"If we Turned . . . ," Leo said tentatively.

Gus knew immediately what he meant. "Eww, gross, Leo!"

"It wouldn't be gross if you were a seal," he pointed out. "It would be breakfast."

"We do need to eat," Gus admitted.

They sat down at the edge of the pool.

Gus closed her eyes and thought about the sea, how it smelled, and sounded, and how the cool water felt closing around her sleek seal body. She felt Leo take her hand. She remembered the sharp smell of mussels clinging to rocks, and the heavier, oxygen-laced odor of the deeper water. Then she remembered the sound of a school of fish skittering anxiously away from her, and the tremendously slow thumping of her own heart when she dove. She followed that sound, its slow beat pulling her deeper and deeper, her nostrils flaring at the rising scent of salt.

Gus strained her entire body forward without moving an inch. She just leaned inside her body. It was like leaning over the edge of a cliff, feeling the movement deep in her muscles and bones, leaning out over the endless drop until she could go no farther. Then something yanked her with tremendous force, an invisible pair of hands that smoothed her from head to foot, and then she was falling forward, over the invisible cliff and into the waiting pool. She heard Leo cry out and then the cool water took her in and welcomed her back.

Gus stretched and rolled in delight. It was so good to be a seal again! Leo rolled next to her, laughing. A small school of round, silvery-pink porgies swam under Gus and Leo. The two seals dove and then surfaced almost immediately with flopping fish in their jaws. They ate the porgies and then went back down for more. As seals, they didn't stop to wonder how a school of ocean-dwelling fish had ended up in the pool. They just feasted.

Gus was diving for the third time when she saw Leo chasing a larger fish, a haddock or a pollack. The fish darted out of sight, and Leo dove deep, deeper than he should have been able to. Then he disappeared.

Chirping frantically, Gus dove after Leo, just in time to see him swim into a dark hole in the side of the pool. With a flick of her tail, she followed. It was pitch-black, but Gus could feel with her whiskers that they were in a tunnel, and that it was wide enough for two seals to swim side by side. She thrust forward and caught up with Leo, who was still chasing the fleeing fish.

As she moved, Gus noticed other tunnels branching off from the one in which they swam. She didn't have time to wonder about them, though—Leo was still swimming hard after the fish, and she had to hurry to keep up with him. They swam together for a minute or so, and then the tunnel abruptly angled upward and dumped them out into open water.

The two seals popped up. "No fish," Leo barked.

"New water," Gus barked back.

This new pool was still in the woods, but it was much larger than the first one. Lacy ferns grew all around its edges, shielding it from sight.

"Many ways to go," Gus said, trying to explain the tunnels she had seen, branching off in various directions.

"Follow one to Ila," Leo suggested.

And so they did, diving and swimming and following one tunnel after another. All the pools on the island seemed to be connected. It must be how the Dobhar-chú traveled from place to place, they decided. Leo reminded Gus that the Dobhar-chú, besides living underwater, could tunnel through rock. The idea of the monster creating the tunnels through which they now swam made Gus shudder. And the thought of meeting up with the King of the Black Lakes in one of the dark underground tunnels made her so nervous that she accidentally Turned and for a moment was a girl splashing in a freezing cold pool of salt water.

But they met no one on their travels. Just fish, and once a small squid, which filled the water around them with a panicked squirt of ink before making its escape.

Then, late in the afternoon, Gus shot up for a breath in a new pool. As she surfaced, she could see that this pool lay not in the woods but at the edge of a meadow. In front of her the trees gave way abruptly, without first thinning and changing to oak or beech, the way they do in most forests. This forest just came to a halt: dark pines against waving, pale green grasses.

Leo popped to the surface and hung next to Gus. "What?" he barked.

Gus flopped her way out of the pool and onto the forest floor. Shrugging her heavy shoulders, she Turned and was a girl sitting on a bed of pine needles. Leo flopped out, Turned, and sat next to her.

"There's a building," Gus said.

She noticed, as she spoke, that she felt much, much better. Her stomach was full, her cuts and scrapes had all been rinsed with salt water, and her head felt clear. The bandage had fallen off her arm, but the wound had stopped bleeding. Leo looked better too. His face had lost its sickly pallor.

In the center of the meadow stood the remains of a stone building. Through the bottom of two rows of arched spaces that might have been doorways or tall windows, they saw a gray stone floor and, visible through the top row, blue sky.

"Let's check it out," Leo said.

They crossed the meadow to where the building stood. The only sound around them was the lazy hum of insects and the grasses shifting in a light breeze. As they got closer, they could see that brambly bushes twined around the outside of the ghostly, broken wreck, climbing up the walls to head height in some places.

"What do you think it is?" Gus whispered.

"A church?" Leo guessed. "A fort? Let's go in."

"No," Gus said. The crumbling building suddenly looked dark and menacing. Its jagged roofline seemed to leer at them in the still air.

"The breeze is gone," Gus said, still whispering. And then she noticed that the sounds of crickets and the rising calls of insects had ceased as well. The meadow lay as silent and still as if it had been buried under a heavy fall of snow.

"I don't like it," she said. "Let's get out of here."

"No," Leo whispered. "Something's here. Can't you feel it?"

"Yeah, and that's why I want to go," Gus hissed, tugging on her twin's hand.

Ignoring her, Leo pulled aside brambles to climb up and into one of the tall window spaces. Gus looked around the empty meadow and then reluctantly followed him in. The thorns caught at her as she did.

"Ow," she whispered, wiping at the stinging places on her legs. Her hands came back with blood on them. She dropped down into the surprisingly dark space next to Leo.

Even with entire pieces of the roof missing, the sunlight did not reach the room. It smelled of mildew and rot and something darker and heavier underneath the more familiar smells.

"Phew, it really stinks in here!" Leo said. "Like BO but way worse."

Gus's foot touched something soft, and as her eyes adjusted to the gloom she could see it was the ripped red pelt of a rabbit. The rotten stink in the room seemed even stronger now that she could see what it was from.

"I want to get out of here," she said.

"I think it was a church," Leo said, ignoring Gus.

It did seem to be a church, as it was a single open space with a raised platform at one end. Here and there, broken chunks of rocks lay where they had fallen from the walls. As they moved slowly around the room, Gus felt something crunching under her feet like dry twigs in a forest. Looking down, she stifled a scream when she realized that she was walking on bones. The entire floor was strewn with them—fish skeletons, but also what looked like rabbits and field mice, and then, to her horror, she saw a human skull lying amid the other bones. She let out a tiny moan.

"Look at this," Leo called quietly to her.

"Leo," Gus said urgently, "I think these are human—"

But Leo was not listening to her. He was at the far end of the room, under a stone arch. Gus hurried after him. She did not want to be alone in this place.

Under the arch shone a large, still pool of water. In the half-light its surface looked thick and black. Gus instinctively took a step back, and then another.

"Should we try it?" Leo said.

Gus shook her head. "I don't know. If she's not there . . ." Her voice trailed off.

She and Leo stared into the pool. Its oily surface gave off an ugly, sullen gleam. Gus shuddered. "Ugh."

"We have to try," Leo said.

Gus nodded. "OK," she said. "Let's Turn."

Their seal bodies saved their lives. As soon as they entered the water, a powerful current yanked them down and flipped them end over end, like sticks caught in a whirlpool. They were thrust into another tunnel. This one was much longer than the others. Even as seals they were pushed to the very end of their air reserves. Gus and Leo thrashed their powerful bodies, moving faster and faster in the darkness. They swept the water for other tunnels, but there was nothing branching off from this one. Then finally the water thrust Gus upward and flung her, huffing and gasping, to the surface. Leo's sleek head popped up next to her. He drew in three great gulps of air.

They were back in the sea. They had surfaced in a tide pool that had formed between slabs of rough, barnacle-covered basalt. A seagull perched at the edge of the pool, cocking his head to observe the two seals, first with one bright eye and then the other.

The shoreline consisted of the same jagged rocks and crashing waves as the place where they had come ashore. Here, however, a long, flat rock reached out above the water like a jetty. At the very tip, tucked into a hollow smoothed by hundreds of years of waves breaking, slumped Ila, dirt-streaked in her soaking wet nightgown. And below her, something swam back and forth in the water, just under the surface, something dark and massive and unmistakably evil.

CHAPTER 24

The King of the Black Lakes

At the sight of their sister, both Leo and Gus burst out of their seal bodies in the freezing tide pool. Instantly, color rushed in—the red of Ila's nightgown, the navy blue of the dusky sky, and the crimson sun lowering itself toward the fog that surrounded the island.

Leo grabbed Gus's shoulder and yanked her down in the pool. His teeth were chattering as he hissed at her.

"Stay down! The Dobhar-chú's in the water."

"I know!" Gus whispered back. "We have to get Ila!"

Instead of answering, Leo Turned. With one last glance at the dark rock and her sister on it, Gus Turned and sank below the surface. Leo was waiting for her.

"You human and I swim," he twittered.

Gus was confused. Surely Leo didn't mean to swim in the water with that creature?

"I swim," he said again. "You run. Get Ila."

"No!" Gus said. "No, no, no! We Turn and run. Get

Ila . . ." Her voice trailed away. There was nothing else to say. They had no plan for killing the monstrous creature that swam so close to their sister. "Wait for Móraí," she said, finally.

Leo hung silently in the water. His dark, round eyes looked sad.

"Wait for Móraí," Gus said again.

Slowly, Leo nodded, and they swam to the surface, Turned, and slipped out of the tide pool. Crouching low, they began to edge toward the long rock. As they moved, Gus caught sight of what looked like a pile of clothing heaped under a low rock. With a shock, she recognized the Bedell's overcoat and realized, in the same second, that the pile *was* the Bedell. With an effort, she forced herself to look away from the broken heap that had been the dapper little Messenger. She needed to focus on Ila. But her eyes blurred with tears as she followed Leo.

Then a voice stopped them. "Well, hello and welcome," said the Dobhar-chú.

Gus and Leo froze on their hands and knees behind a cluster of boulders.

"So noisy underwater," the voice continued. "All that chitchat. Not very sneaky, are you, little sea dumplings? Now come out and show yourselves. If you value your sister's life, that is."

Gus and Leo stood up and looked out across the water. Directly below Ila, just breaking the surface of the sea, was the great head of the Dobhar-chú. It was much, much bigger than they had imagined it would be. Dark, leathery skin stretched over bone like a thing out of a museum, some ancient monster that once roamed the earth. The head turned toward them and then rose out of the water on a long serpent's neck. They could see gills fluttering on either side of its muzzle and down to where the creature disappeared into the water. The King of the Black Lakes observed them with unblinking eyes the color of hot tar.

"Come closer," he said.

Neither Gus nor Leo could move. They were pinned down by horror and fear like specimens in a display case. Gus thought about the creature's claws, hidden by the water, that could tunnel through rock.

The creature stretched out its thick, long neck and nuzzled Ila gently in a parody of tenderness.

"No!" Gus screamed.

She and Leo ran, stumbling and falling, to the long, dark rock where their sister slumped. But as soon as they reached the end of the rock, the Dobhar-chú spoke again. "That is close enough, I think."

"Ila!" Gus said desperately. "Ila, we're here!" Her entire body was trembling with the effort it took to keep from running to her little sister.

Ila did not respond. They could see now that her eyes were closed. And at least some of the dirt on her face was actually an ugly purple bruise.

"Ila?" Gus said, her voice breaking.

The King of the Black Lakes opened his jaws to Gus and Leo, showing them row after row of jagged teeth. "I suppose I don't *have* to kill her," he said, and winked. The gesture was grotesque on the bony face.

Leo lunged forward, but Gus grabbed the bottom of his T-shirt and held him next to her.

"Not yet," she murmured. They just needed to wait for the Móraí to arrive. Surely all of them together could fight the monster.

"But I do so want to!" the Dobhar-chú said merrily. "And, you know," he added, lowering his voice as if to tell them a secret, "you are Folk, after all. Must wipe you all out, I'm afraid. And then, I suppose, more killing, more fear, more despair. Much, much more. What fun it will be!"

"Ila?" Gus whispered. She could feel the tears running down her face.

The creature showed his teeth in a snarl. "Now," he said, "where is the old woman?"

"She's on her way!" Leo said angrily.

"Well, then," the creature said, settling himself down in the water like a cat on a cushion. "In that case, we shall just have to make ourselves comfortable and wait. It would be such a shame to kill you three and still be stuck in this place. With her gone, I can finally see a bit of the world!"

"Gills," Leo murmured.

"What?" Gus tried to speak without moving her mouth. Every cell in her body was screaming to her to get to Ila, to run and snatch her little sister out of this place.

"He's half Femori, and he has gills," Leo whispered. "That means he needs the sea. The Femorians couldn't leave the water. It would kill them. He's only half, but we need to get him out of the water, Gus."

"Great," Gus muttered.

"What's that?" the Dobhar-chú called. "No whispers, little sea slugs. So impolite."

But as the Dobhar-chú spoke, Gus's attention was caught by something beyond the monstrous creature. Out to sea, the fog bank was shifting. For a few wonderful seconds, she thought that it was the Móraí arriving.

But then Leo said, "Oh no," in a soft voice so full of grief that Gus knew what she was really seeing. The fog was lifting.

It shimmered like a curtain in a light breeze, and then it began to thin. The setting sun, which had disappeared behind the bank, glowed through the increasingly transparent skin, staining the sea red.

The Móraí was not coming to help them. They were on their own. The three of them against the creature in the sea, who now turned his head to follow the spreading light on the water.

"Oh, I think the game has changed," the Dobhar-chú said quietly. "It seems you are all alone, my small friends."

The Dobhar-chú gazed down at Ila where she half sat, half lay on the cold stone, and his glowing dark eyes shifted from black to burgundy to incandescent red.

"Here I come, little fox," he whispered.

The wind had dropped to the stillness just before dusk. It was so quiet, with no seagulls shrieking or waves crashing against the rocks. The sea had gone purple, and the lowering sun gilded the air around them, lighting Ila's pale throat.

Leo began to run.

Gus knew he would never get there in time. So she did the only thing she could think of. She stepped forward, opened her mouth, and began to speak. "On this night," she said. Her voice was a small, thin thing, just a thread hanging in the air. "This darkest hour," she said, her voice gaining strength. "This hearth, / This house, / This hold."

Leo had reached Ila. Kneeling down, he gathered her in his arms, shielding her with his body. Above them, the Dobhar-chú's head on its long neck was poised to strike, but something held him. His eyes turned slowly back to black, an inky stain that spread over the red like darkness overtaking fire.

"No," he said, but his voice was a whisper.

Gus's voice was loud and strong now, calling out the poem easily, remembering the words as though she had heard them every night of her life:

> On the fire
> On the bower
> On the young
> And old.

As she spoke, the Dobhar-chú roared, and the sound rolled out and across the rocks, knocking Leo and Ila over. Gus staggered backward and then began to run to her brother and sister.

As she reached them, the Dobhar-chú roared again. There was no blocking out the sound of his fury. It blasted into their bodies and shook the air around them, pressing them to the ground and filling the night with desolation, and terror, and endless hunger. Covering their ears did no good. The sound came in through their skin, their eyes, and worked its way between the fingers they had pressed over their ears.

Out of nowhere, a driving rain began to fall, soaking the children and obscuring their vision. Thunder rolled across the ocean. Gus moaned in fear as a jagged lightning bolt zigzagged down over the rock on which they crouched. Another bolt lit the sky and illuminated the King of the Black Lakes. Higher and higher the creature rose, a nightmare of darkness and fury. His head whipped back and forth on his long, thick neck as water rolled off his body in sheets. Another lightning bolt lit the sky as he threw back his head and roared, his mouth growing wider and wider. A second set of jaws pushed forward from his mouth, thrashing and wailing and baring its own set of jagged teeth.

Crouched on the wet rock with Leo and Ila, who still had not opened her eyes, Gus gasped out the rest of the poem, forcing the words out against the driving rain and the slashing wind:

From the forest
From the fen
From the flame
And sea,
Salt and iron
Rock and den
To fight
To shield,
The three.

Suddenly the creature in the sea went quiet. The storm fled, as abruptly as it had appeared. The night was falling fast now, with a fat, full moon rising up over the edge of the dark horizon. Soon the moon would light the water, but for now the Dobhar-chú was just a dark shadow. The second set of jaws clacked and hissed inside his mouth.

Gus huddled on the rock. She could feel Leo's arms around her and Ila. She thought she could feel her sister's heart beating. She had a sudden flash of anger with the Móraí, for sending them against this monster with nothing but a poem as defense. Shouldn't they have had weapons of some sort? Now they were as helpless as rabbits spotted on the ground by a sharp-eyed eagle, their only options to freeze or to run.

The moon found its place in the sky, throwing a line of light across the water that illuminated the Dobhar-chú. He was bent low in the water and it seemed, for a moment, that he had been wounded badly by the words of the night poem. But as they watched, he began to straighten out his neck, rolling his head from side to side like a beast shaking off a blow.

"We have to run," Leo whispered, although they both knew that it was too late for that. They could not run fast enough to escape the Dobhar-chú, especially not while carrying Ila.

"The book, Leo!" Gus hissed. "What else did the book say?"

Leo frantically ran through everything he had read in the book. The creatures who fought for the Dobhar-chú, the ones who had taken the side of the Folk, and the ones who had refused to fight at all, returning instead to the deeps, where they were lost to the world . . .

"Lost!" Leo said out loud. "Lost to the world! Gus, I don't think we're the Lost Children after all! I think the final stanza is about the sea creatures! We need to call them!"

"But I don't remember the last stanza!" Gus said desperately.

"Something about three," Leo said. "And dark, oh I don't remember!"

Then a voice spoke. It was not loud, but it was familiar. It was the Bedell. He was alive, wearing his ripped and stained overcoat, standing behind them on the long rock. His face was deadly pale in the moonlight, and he spoke with great effort, as though the words themselves were causing him terrible pain.

"I will help you," he said, and then bent double with his hands on his knees.

"Silence, Messenger!" the Dobhar-chú roared. He heaved in the water but did not move forward.

Still bent double, the small man said, "I am so sorry, children. I was a fool." Then he straightened up and called out to the creature in the water, "I am not of the Folk, King. It was you yourself that reminded me of this. I will never be one of them. But I will never serve you either."

The man stepped forward and laid his hands on Ila's forehead.

"No!" Gus cried out.

"Ila," the Bedell said urgently. "Ila, you must wake. Your brother and sister need you, child. Please."

"Stop it!" Gus cried out. "You've hurt her enough!" She leapt forward, yanking at the Bedell's overcoat to get him away from her sister, but then Ila stirred in Leo's arms.

Without opening her eyes, Ila murmured, "This eve."

"Ila?" Leo said in disbelief.

"This eve," Ila said again, very softly.

"That's right," Gus said. "That's the beginning, Leo. She's right!"

"Can you say more?" Leo asked Ila. "Ila, can you say the rest?"

The Bedell stepped away and sank to his knees as Ila spoke again.

"This night / This endless night," she whispered.

Then, opening her eyes, which glowed a bright, pure green, she spoke the rest of the poem, carefully and clearly.

> *Three is many*
> *Weak is might*
> *Call the creatures*
> *To the light*
> *Oh, Lost Children, come.*

Shaking off Leo's embrace, Ila stood and, spreading her arms wide, she called out the last line of the poem one more time. When she spoke the words, two things happened: she shimmered into the form of a red fox, and the Dobhar-chú dove, screaming, as the words from the poem reached across the water for him. And when the monster surfaced again, he was not alone.

CHAPTER 25

The Lost Children

The little fox howled, a long, high sound that stretched up and into the night sky.

The darkness of the night was lit by the full moon, and below it, the surface of the sea was alive with motion, eddies and whirlpools and waves rising out of nothing. It might have been sharks, but no fins cut the surface of the roiling water. *Something* was out there, though—the Dobhar-chú was spinning and twisting like a stag with hounds worrying its every step. But there were no black-and-white leaping bodies and no quick silvery dolphins. Ila had called something else.

Leo and Gus found themselves on their feet, each with a hand bunched in the fur of the fox, who strained forward toward the water.

"What is it?" Gus shouted.

"I don't know!" Leo shouted back, tightening his grip on Ila's fur.

They heard a scream from the water that sounded like that of a woman, and then a cry that began as the whinny of a horse and ended as the howling of a beast. A long breaker rolled across the sea, smashing near the struggling Dobhar-chú. In the foam of the breaking wave, the children could see what looked like men, at least a dozen of them, all with dark hair and skin and tridents gripped in their hands.

"Finfolk!" Leo cried.

The finfolk dove under the surface. The Dobhar-chú roared and heaved and slashed at the dark water where they had disappeared.

As the Dobhar-chú fought, the water in front of the children split open in a V shape, like the wake that follows a boat. At the head of the V was a horse, swimming strongly, and on its back sat a woman with flowing pale hair.

Ila snarled as the horse approached. Gus could feel the fox trembling under her fingers.

"That horse is a kelpie," Leo whispered.

Ila snarled again.

The kelpie stopped just short of where the breakers smashed on the rocks. This close they could see the curve of its long incisors, more like fangs than teeth. It shook its mane and screamed, rolling back its black lips to bare its teeth at them.

"You called us!" the woman sang out from the back of the plunging creature. Her hair flowed around her like a silver cape made of moonlight and seaweed.

It was unclear if it was a question or a statement, but Leo stepped forward.

"Yes!" Leo shouted across the breaking waves. "That is, my sister called you."

Ila leaned toward Leo, whining, but Gus kept a firm grip on the little fox. She did not want her sister anywhere near the creature in the water.

"And we have come," the woman said. She spoke at a normal volume now, but her voice, high and sweet and indescribably lovely, carried effortlessly across the water. Gus felt her chest tighten with longing at the sound of it. In front of her, Leo took another step forward, and then another. With a wrench, Ila tore free from Gus and raced around Leo, crowding him like a sheepdog, forcing him away from the water.

The woman on the pony's back laughed, a light, liquid, watery sound.

"Do not fear us tonight," she sang out. "We have come at your call."

With that, she wheeled the kelpie around, and together, beast and woman dove underneath the surface. Gus could see, as the pony dove, that the woman sat as though in an old-fashioned sidesaddle. But she had no saddle, and where her legs should have been there was a scaled tail, shimmering in the moonlight. Then she was gone and Gus could breathe again.

Gus ran to Leo and Ila. Now they could see that the foamy breakers in the water were actually the manes of the carnivorous kelpies. Each one bore a mermaid or a finman on its back. The mermaids' pale hair streamed out behind them as they rode. They carried no weapons, but their plunging, screaming mounts seemed like deadly weapons themselves. The finmen sat tall and still on their kelpies. Their dark skin and hair blended with the night, so that all the children could see of them were their silver tridents and their flashing teeth. And then, with a great leaping in their hearts, they saw the seals swimming in and among the finfolk and mermaids, seemingly unafraid of the dreadful kelpies. The sea was alive with magical creatures.

The Dobhar-chú was roaring and plunging as he lashed out. He tore a mermaid from her mount and then slashed the snarling kelpie from end to end. Two finmen thrust their tridents toward his side, but the weapons glanced off of the monster. Without ceasing his attack on the mermaids, the Dobhar-chú whipped his tail around and slammed into the two finmen, throwing their broken bodies into the dark sea. A mermaid screamed, high and long, as the Dobhar-chú drove her off her kelpie.

"They can't fight him," Gus said desperately. "He's going to kill them all!"

But the creatures were not fighting back. Those that were not cut down by the monster were swimming around the Dobhar-chú in a wide ring, faster and faster, seals and kelpies alongside mermaids and finfolk. The Dobhar-chú spun and bellowed in fury, like a great caged bear being baited by dogs. And still the creatures swam, faster and faster, trapping the Dobhar-chú in a ring of water that began to swirl and spin and take shape.

"It's a whirlpool!" Leo shouted. The water sped up and began to take on a distinct funnel shape, with the Dobhar-chú at the center. As the whirlpool grew, the Dobhar-chú began to tilt, pulled by the inexorably spinning vortex. Then, all at once, the King of the Black Lakes was yanked under by the water, roaring and thrashing as he went. The creatures, as one, dove with him.

The children were left in the moonlit night, alone on the rock. The Messenger was nowhere to be seen. The sea was flat, and calm, and still.

"The Lost Children, Gus!" Leo said excitedly. "Don't you see? That's why we had to come back! We were to call the creatures back! *The Book of the Folk* said they were lost to the world. That's what it meant. And that's what the last stanza in the poem means. That's why the book showed it to us!"

Ila, still in her fox form, whined uneasily.

"Do you think—" Gus started to say, but that was all she got out, because with a sound like a rushing tornado, a geyser of water reached up into the night sky. The Dobhar-chú exploded out of the geyser, spit out with such force that he was hurled over the water, landing in a heap on the rocks.

With a scream, the fox made for him.

"Ila, no!" Gus shouted. She glanced at the water, but the creatures were gone. They were on their own.

"Come on, Gus," Leo gasped, starting to run after Ila.

The Dobhar-chú lay wedged between two chunks of rock. As he rocked back and forth, attempting to get free, they could see his body for the first time. While his giant, bony head was leathery skin, the rest of the Dobhar-chú was covered in wet, glistening black scales. His front legs were short and strong, ending in claws that shone like diamonds in the moonlight. He began to dig with his gigantic claws, tunneling into the rock. But being out of the water was affecting him already. His scales were dulling and his breath was coming in short, hard gasps.

The fox was dodging in and out, barking and snapping at the creature, keeping him from concentrating on his digging. With a wide swing of his tail, he knocked her, yelping, off her feet. Then, with a great wrench, the Dobhar-chú yanked his body free from the rocks and attempted to leap after Ila. But as he opened his mouth, he released a great gout of oily, stinking dark liquid. He staggered backward. His second set of jaws hung limply from his gaping mouth, and a half-dozen teeth clattered onto the rocks below him. The creature swung his head sharply from side to side, like a snake feeling the air for prey, and then moved again toward the little fox, who was on her feet, hissing and spitting, her tail a stiff, angry brush behind her.

As he moved, the twins leapt together for the Dobhar-chú, their leaps turning midair into the sleek dives of seals.

Seals, although they may look gentle, are ferocious

hunters. Leo bared his sharp, pointed front teeth as he leapt, and Gus did the same. Leo landed on the creature first. Lunging for the Dobhar-chú's head, he caught it high on the neck. Gus grabbed the tail, which whipped around frantically.

The Dobhar-chú fought them, writhing under their gripping teeth, slamming Gus into a rock so hard that her vision went dark for a moment. The seals clung desperately to the fighting creature. Leo's hold on his throat was restricting the creature's breath, and gradually, his lunges and twists weakened.

But while Gus and Leo didn't release their grip on the creature, they did not move to kill him either, because they had remembered the same thing: That whoever killed the Dobhar-chú would also die.

In those few, endless seconds, Gus saw Leo in his G&T classroom, his head turning in answer to her silent call. Then she saw Ila the way she had first seen her, in their mother's arms, peering up at them suspiciously with eyes that were lit with green light. Then she saw herself in the bath, floating underwater, listening to her parents' voices downstairs, their familiar, ordinary, wonderful voices. Gus closed her eyes, letting herself listen one last time. Then she released the tail and lunged for Leo, knocking him away from the Dobhar-chú, so that she could close her own teeth on his slick black neck. But the little fox was faster. Ila got there first.

Ila was a blur of fur as she dove under Gus. The force of Gus's own lunge knocked Leo off the Dobhar-chú, and the two of them rolled to one side. They leapt together for the fox, their combined weight barreling into her, and the three of them slid across the wet rock, the fox's teeth still gripping the Dobhar-chú's throat and the seals trying desperately to break her hold. The Dobhar-chú lashed its thick tail like a bullwhip, pummeling Gus and Leo. Just then, a sleek form shot across the rocks, its teeth bared in a snarl. It was the Messenger.

The sea mink slashed viciously at the fox, who screamed in surprise and pain. For just a moment, Ila loosened her hold on the monster, and as she did, the mink slid into her place, closing his razor-sharp teeth on the Dobhar-chú's neck, just behind the snapping jaws.

The struggle was bloody and terrible. The mink hung on grimly, even as the Dobhar-chú whipped his powerful body back and forth, smashing the clinging sea mink against the rocks. Then the Dobhar-chú's second set of jaws shot out of its mouth and fastened on the back of the sea mink.

The mink let out a muffled scream as the jaws ground down through flesh and into bone. His legs kicked spasmodically as the jaws reached his backbone, but still he did not release his grip on the Dobhar-chú's neck. The Dobhar-chú let out a long, gurgling wail, and then the second set of jaws released the mink as well as a gout of the Dobhar-chú's black blood, and with one final twitch, the Dobhar-chú was still. The mink released its grip and collapsed on the rock next to the dead monster.

Ila Turned back into a child. With blood running

from three parallel gashes on one cheek, she went to the sea mink, crouching low and stroking its head.

Gus and Leo, still seals, watched as the mink's beautiful coat shimmered once in the moonlight. Then Ila was kneeling at the side of the Bedell in his torn and bleeding human form, his eyes closed in his chalk-white face. Ila leaned close and whispered something in the man's ear. He smiled slightly and opened his eyes, and then, looking directly at Ila, the Messenger died.

The silence around them was immense, encompassing the night sky and the scattering of late stars wheeling over their heads. Ila took a deep, shuddering breath. As they watched, wisps of smoke began to rise up around the man, enveloping him. But although the wisps moved like smoke, they whispered like creatures. It was just possible to see the shapes of sea minks as they wound around the Bedell. The dark shadows sighed and swirled and settled on the Messenger, covering his body like a cloak. Then, abruptly, there was nothing there but the darkness, laid as flat on the rock as a blanket stretched tightly over an empty bed.

Gus and Leo Turned. Leo took off his T-shirt, and Gus used it to wipe the blood from Ila's face.

"I'm fine," Ila said, squirming away from Gus's touch, just like the old Ila would have. The three of them stood for a moment as the moon began its descent. The long night was coming to an end.

"Home," Ila said.

Gus nodded. She was trying not to look at the torn

body of the monster lying on the rock. She could smell it, though, a stench of rancid oil and blood.

"Yes," she said, her stomach rolling over. "Let's get out of here."

"We don't have the boat," Leo said.

"I know where it is," Ila said. Her hair seemed to brighten as she spoke, and then she was sitting on her haunches, a fox once again, gazing up at them.

Ila led them quickly and surely over the moonlit rocks to where the skidbladnin lay abandoned. Without speaking, they climbed aboard the little boat, Ila a child again, and Leo pushed them off and into the sea.

As the boat began to move, Gus closed her eyes. The face of the Móraí rose up in her mind, indescribably old, her bright eyes gentle and sad. And next to her, the Messenger, in his overcoat and his fingerless gloves. As she watched, they both smiled. When Ila took her hand, she opened her eyes and turned to face the open sea. The boat knew where it was going, and they slipped through the water as though in a dream, moving without thought, just motion.

CHAPTER 26

Home

They woke to a sea on fire. It was morning, and the sun was just rising. They had to squint against the vivid intensity of the reflected light.

As the boat neared the shore of Loup Marin, Gus took in the fire of the sun on the water, the quick dartings of fish just under the surface, and the sound like a heartbeat that was the ocean itself, breathing in time with her. Without thinking or planning, she Turned and slipped off the boat into the welcoming water. With a bark, Leo splashed down next to her, and then the red fox leapt into the water as well, paddling in circles around the delighted seals. Leo and Gus dove and rolled in the still water, and then they popped up and swam slowly to shore, side by side with the paddling fox.

The seals Turned and splashed through the shallows to the rocky beach, where they lay down to dry their wet clothes in the morning sunlight.

Ila was still a fox. She sat nearby, with slight wisps of steam rising off her red coat. Her tongue was out, and Gus could have sworn that she was laughing.

Ignoring the little fox, Gus rolled onto her stomach and closed her eyes. Leo joined her, and it was some time before they opened their eyes. When they did, Ila was a little girl again, sitting near them making a wobbly tower of small rocks.

"Let's go to the house," she said.

Grief clutched at Gus's heart when they reached the small cottage.

The bright blue door was faded and hung open on broken hinges. The carving of the leaping fish on the door was just visible as faint, gray scratches in the peeling blue paint. Gus laid her hand over the fish, but she already knew what she would find. The image was cold and still. Inside, the cozy living room with its lamps and brightly colored couch and piles of cushions was chilly and dark. A stiff sea wind blew in through a broken window. The lamps were in pieces on the floor along with small bones that looked like they might have belonged to mice. The couch was shredded and the low coffee table broken on the blue woven rug, which was covered in mold.

They moved around slowly, touching things, remembering, and silently mourning the old woman who had fed, cared for, and died for them in the end.

"The book!" Leo suddenly remembered. They searched among the piles of ripped and tattered books that littered the floor. But *The Book of the Folk* was gone.

"I'm sorry, Leo," Gus said.

Leo stood with his back to her, his shoulders shaking just a bit. Gus knew it wasn't just the book. It was everything. The ruined house, the lost Móraí, and the missing book, with its glorious stories and memories and links to a family they had never known they had.

"It's all lost," Leo said.

"But not us," Ila said.

Leo shook his head. He pulled off his glasses and wiped his eyes. "I'm going to the lighthouse," he said as he shoved his glasses back on.

He left, and Gus and Ila went into the kitchen.

Spiders scuttled from the dry sink when Gus tried to turn on the water. The oven door of the cast-iron stove hung open on its rusty hinges. Inside was a frothy mouse nest made of grass and what looked like shreds of the curtains that used to hang in the girls' room. The damp sea air blew forlornly through the house, ruffling the dust that lay over everything.

After a while, Gus left Ila in the bedroom, where she insisted on searching for Bear, and went to the lighthouse to check on Leo.

Inside the lighthouse everything had changed. In the watch room, the bed with the bright blue quilt was gone, as were the telescope and the rocking chair where the Móraí had sat on her night watches.

In the lantern room, the beautiful Fresnel lens was shattered, the floor around it strewn with bits of glass that glittered in the sunlight.

"What's happened?" Leo said when Gus came into the room. He was standing in front of the ruined Fresnel lens. When he moved, the reflected light from the shards on the floor winked on his glasses. "What's going on?"

"Maybe we were gone for years," Gus said, panic beginning at the edges of her mind. "Maybe everyone is . . . gone."

They stared at one another in horror. Everyone gone? Their parents, old and buried? Their classmates adults, or perhaps even older than that, perhaps also grown old and died without ever knowing what had become of the Brennan children, who had all disappeared without a trace when they were young? Gus sat down on the floor next to Leo. Her head was spinning. Just then, Ila came into the room carrying something. It was her bear.

"Bear is fine," she announced, and indeed he was, his fur as soft and new as before, his overalls fresh and clean, without any dust on them.

"I found our backpacks too," Ila said. She led them back to the house, to the little bedroom where the girls had slept. The mattresses had been pulled from the beds and shredded, as had all the bedding, which lay in a filthy, ruined heap on the floor. But in the closet lay two backpacks. Like the bear, they were fresh and clean.

Leo came in carrying his backpack. "And look," he said, pulling out his watch from the front pocket, where he had tucked it for safekeeping when they left the motel in the middle of the night with the Bedell, so long ago, it now seemed. It was an old watch, handed down from Pop Brennan to their father to Leo, that required winding.

"It hasn't run down," Leo pointed out. He showed the girls the face of the watch where, sure enough, the hands were ticking steadily. Carefully Leo tucked the watch into the pocket of his jeans.

"And food!" Gus said triumphantly. She pulled the sandwiches that the Mórai had made for her and Ila out of her backpack. They were fresh, the bread not even stale. There was also a bottle of water.

"Starving!" Leo said.

They fell on the food, which was made even more wonderful by the discovery of four oatmeal cookies tucked in the bottom of Gus's pack. For a while, the only sound was contented chewing.

"Phew," Gus said. She wiped a bit of honey off her lip. "That feels better. I guess we're still in our time, right? If the sandwiches are still good? I was afraid—" She laughed unsteadily. "But if it's not a hundred years later, then what happened here?"

"I think," said Leo thoughtfully, "I think the magic—that is, the Mórai, and the Messenger—isn't here anymore. So without them, the house is—"

"Ruined?" Gus said skeptically.

"No," Leo said. "Not ruined. Just old. The way it

really is. The way it would be if the Móraí had not been keeping it young."

They all remembered the frail old woman standing before the howling, snarling wolf pack. Tears came to Gus's eyes.

"Let's go back to the beach," Ila said.

So they retraced their steps to the rocky shore. The water was flat and calm. The sun was high in the sky and the afternoon was very warm. After a while, all three of the children fell asleep on the warm black rocks.

Gus was awakened by a sound like someone blowing out a great whoosh of air. She knew before she opened her eyes what it was, but her delight was still sharp when she saw the seals. They were lying on the flat rocks, floating in the calm sea, and popping up in the water like gophers in a pasture, here, there, everywhere, with the whooshing sound that had awakened Gus.

"Ila, Leo, wake up!" Gus said as her brother and sister stirred and then, with cries of delight, took in the creatures all around them. Ila shimmered just slightly, her red hair looking for a moment like fur lying close to her head, but then it faded and she was just Ila again, laughing at a baby seal who had shoved its nose into her outstretched hand like a curious puppy.

Suddenly the seals grew still, and then, as though at a signal, they all slipped off the rocks and into the water. They hung there, silent and watchful, their large eyes just visible. Another seal was approaching. As it broke the surface near the edge of the closest rock, they could see that it was not the bright white of the baby seals or the richer brown of the older ones. This seal was lustrous silver, the color of the moon on a cloudless night in winter. It was swimming very slowly. When it came closer, they could see why—it bore several unhealed gashes on one side of its body. The seal's right eye was gone, the skin around the empty eye socket bloodied and torn by sharp teeth that had gouged and bitten.

"It's the Mórai," Ila said softly.

"Oh!" Gus said, feeling a rush of joy so strong she had to sit down to keep her balance.

One by one, they each went to the seal.

Gus went last. The seal's nose was wet and soft in her palm. When she looked into its one remaining eye, she knew that Ila was right. And she knew that the seal was saying thank you.

"You're welcome," she whispered.

The seal swam back to Ila and looked into her green eyes with its one brown eye.

"She's sorry she couldn't come to us," Ila said softly. "But she can take us home, if we go slowly. And she wants—ugh—she wants me to be a big, stinky seal."

"How do you know that?" Leo asked.

Ila shrugged. "I just do."

"Can you be a seal?" Gus asked.

"She says yes," Ila reported. "I say yuck."

Leo laughed. "Just try it, Ila. You might like it."

Ila looked more like a fox than ever as her hair flared red and the green starbursts in her eyes lit up and spread over the brown.

"Fine," she said. With a sigh, she shrugged her shoulders, and then, sitting before them was a very small seal. Its body was a creamy white with light splotches that shaded to dark fur at its head and back flippers. Its face was a mask of creamy white fur, and its eyes, rather than the soft brown of a seal, were incandescent green.

"You're not supposed to be able to do that until you're eleven," Leo pointed out mildly. The seal let out a bark that sounded like laughter.

"She's special," Gus said, making quotation marks in the air. She was smiling as she shrugged into what was starting to feel like her real body, the one that waited under her human body like skin under a set of clothes.

The three seals dove into the sea where the wounded seal waited for them.

"Welcome," she said.

There was so much to say! Gus struggled to begin the seal language. But before she could speak again, the old seal began swimming away, slowly but steadily. After a brief hesitation and one last look back at Loup Marin, the three seals followed her. Behind them, the other seals spread out in a loose V, flanking and protecting their journey. Along the way, strange, foamy rollers appeared and disappeared around them. Gus thought she heard a scrap of singing somewhere not very far away, but she could never be sure of that.

*　*　*

They swam through the night, reaching their destination as morning began to pinken the sky and warm the top layer of the water. When the four seals surfaced, they could see a rocky shoreline and, above that, a long lawn that sloped upward to a small white house whose windows all looked out on the sea. In one of the windows stood two figures, waiting.

The Mórai swam to Leo and touched his nose with her own. She did the same to Gus and finally to Ila, who let out a little bark of sadness.

Then, with one last long look that took in the three seals, the rocky shore, and the house with the two human silhouettes in the living room window, the seal drew in a breath and dove. And as she did, all of the other seals did as well, so that the water went from lumpy to as flat and unmoving as a pane of glass.

Gus felt a sharp, keen thing in her heart. She knew they would not see the Mórai again.

Ahead of her, Ila burst out of the water in her human form and began to scramble up the rocks.

Leo and Gus looked at one another and, with a strange feeling that was a mix of joy and loss, they slipped out of their seal shapes and splashed out after their little sister.

"I wonder what we've missed," Leo said as they began to walk slowly up the back lawn. He felt like he was waking from a long, complicated dream.

•270•

"I don't know," Gus said. It seemed so distant. School, friends—all the things of their former lives seemed very far away. *This must be how adults remember childhood,* she thought.

"Do you think we'll ever be able to Turn again?" Gus asked.

"I don't know," Leo said.

Gus felt a pang of loss, and thought one more time of the Móraí, and the little cottage nestled in the shadow of a lighthouse on one of the Far Islands. For a moment, her eyes swam with tears.

Then the back door of the house was flung open and their father burst out, calling their names, and behind him came their mother.

Ila shouted, "Mom!" her voice carrying clearly across the lawn and all the way to the sea. Their mother laughed to hear her speak and then began to weep and took her into her arms. Their father stood next to them with his hand on Ila's head, his eyes on Gus and Leo. Leo took Gus's hand and squeezed it hard. She squeezed back, and then they began to run up the lawn, to where Ila and their parents waited for them.

And in the small library at the back of the house, hidden behind a pile of old and dusty magazines, a brown leather book breathed gently, waiting.

AUTHOR'S NOTE

Selkies, it seems, have been around for as long as we have had stories to tell about them. I started thinking about them several years ago when I saw the film *The Secret of Roan Inish*, about a girl in Ireland who is searching for her brother, Jamie, who she believes was taken by seals when his cradle washed out to sea. That film is based on a novel for children by Rosalie K. Fry called *Secret of the Ron Mor Skerry*. The book is (sadly) out of print, but you might be able to find it at your library.

Selkies (also called silkies or selchies) can be found in the stories of people living near the sea in Ireland, Scotland, England, the Faeroe Islands, and even Iceland. Selkies are "seal people," creatures that can exist in either human or animal form. You may have heard the story of the seal wife, which is told in many different ways and in many cultures: a fisherman finds the sealskin of a selkie woman and steals it, forcing her to come with him and be his wife. Many years later, one of the woman's children finds the sealskin hidden away and asks his mother about it. As soon as the seal wife spots her skin, she rushes to the sea and throws it on, turning instantly back into a seal. The seal wife never returns to land, although many of the stories say that she visits in seal form every so often to bring fish to her human children.

So there I was, thinking about selkies, when I came

across a book at my local library. It was just a small, tattered paperback, but something about it caught my eye. The book was called *The People of the Sea*, written by a man named David Thomson. It recounts Thomson's actual search for tales about the "seal people" among the inhabitants of the coasts and islands of Scotland and Ireland. The book tells of dark-eyed people with webbed fingers, of seals who came into kitchens looking for their lost children, of fishermen rescued from drowning by seals. I signed the book out again and again, and finally got my own copy.

The People of the Sea describes more than selkies. It also tells of a creature that I had never heard of before—the Dobhar-chú, or "King Otter." I started to research the Dobhar-chú—which is pronounced DOO-*wuhr-coo*—and found stories of the creature all over Ireland. Also known as the "water hound" or "hound of the deep," and, occasionally, the "king of the lakes," the Dobhar-chú lives in lakes, rivers, and the depths of the sea, is pure white with a cross of brown on its back, and can tunnel underground through rock and earth. The Dobhar-chú is a cryptid (from the Greek *kryptos*, meaning "hidden")—that is, a creature in whose existence many people believe, although it has not been proved by science (like the Loch Ness monster, the yeti, or . . . selkies!). For those who doubt, there is a grave in a cemetery in County Leitrim, in Ireland, of a woman named Gráinne, who, according to her gravestone, was killed by a Dobhar-chú in the seventeenth century. And an Irish artist named Sean

Corcoran says he saw a Dobhar-chú in 2003 in a lake in Connemara, in County Galway.

I could find no sign of the Dobhar-chú in America, and we do not have many stories of the selkies, even in our coastal towns. So for *Lost Children of the Far Islands,* I decided to bring the selkies and the Dobhar-chú to Maine.

If you want to read more about selkie myths, here are some books that were useful to me:

Myth, Legend, and Romance: An Encyclopedia of the Irish Folk Tradition by Dr. Dáithi Ó hÓgáin

Orkney Folklore and Sea Legends by Walter Traill Dennison

The People of the Sea: A Journey in Search of the Seal Legend by David Thomson

Tales of the Seal People: Scottish Folk Tales by Duncan Williamson, illustrated by Chad McCail

If you want to read more fiction in which selkies are featured, try these books:

The Folk Keeper by Franny Billingsley

Seaward by Susan Cooper

The Selkie and the Fisherman by Chardi Christian, illustrated by Freya Blackwood

Selkie Girl by Laurie Brooks

ACKNOWLEDGMENTS

The idea for this book began in two places: at the Ragdale Foundation Artist's Residency in the form of a conversation about selkies with Brendan Isaac Jones, and within the hallowed walls of the Flying Pig Bookstore in Shelburne, Vermont. Thank you, Ragdale; thank you, Brendan; and thank you, Josie and Elizabeth, for running the best bookstore in America! The actual book was written in many, many places. Thanks to both my parents and my parents-in-law, who offered up quiet places in Vermont and Ireland where I could hole up and write. Thanks also to the Ryan barn in Springs, the Society Library in Manhattan, and the Ost coffee shop in the East Village—you guys may not know it, but I wrote the final draft of this novel in your warm and welcoming space, fired up by your perfect cappuccinos!

My brothers and sisters read drafts, sent encouragement, ran story lines by their own children, and most important, believed in me from the very beginning. I love you guys. Many, many thanks to my agent, George Nicholson, whose enthusiasm for the early draft of this book changed my life. Thanks also to my incredibly talented editor, Michelle Frey, who pushed me (gently) to fill in every gap and do the hard work, and her assistant Kelly Delaney—you two are a great team! And finally, to my husband, Paul, who worked tirelessly on this book as combination Head Cheerleader/Strength Coach: I could not have done it without you.

In writing the story, I drew on a wonderful little book called *The People of the Sea* by David Thomson. *The People of the Sea* gave me not only my seals but my monster as well.

ABOUT THE AUTHOR

Emily Raabe is a writer and poet who lives in New York City with her husband. *Leave It Behind,* her first book of poems, was a finalist for the FutureCycle Poetry Book Prize. She is the author of several nonfiction books for children. *Lost Children of the Far Islands* is her first novel.